# SCANDALOUSLY YOURS

A SWEET ROCK STAR ROM-COM

CELEBRITY LOVE IN NEW ORLEANS
BOOK 1

## KATIE TALBOT

LAKE VISTA
PRESS

Cover design by Beck and Dot Book Covers

Published by Lake Vista Press

978-1-969144-02-8 (ebook)

978-1-969144-03-5 (paperback)

First edition, 2025

Library of Congress Control Number: 202591048

*For my family, who always save the drama for their mama. Thanks for making life as entertaining as any rom-com.*

# 1

## ELIZABETH

EVERY GOOD STORYTELLER KNOWS: never kill the dog.

It was the kind of mistake that didn't just haunt you. It made international headlines.

And the worst part? I was supposed to be the one preventing disasters like that.

I mean, I didn't actually kill Sparky. I accidentally sent out the pre-written press release that said he was dead instead of the one announcing his comeback for Season 10. Sparky was the beloved golden retriever on America's favorite primetime comedy.

My mix-up set off a social media meltdown and an actual candlelight vigil in Central Park.

So, yeah. Not my best day.

I fielded calls from journalists and Sparky's "devastated fans," and crafted the perfect apology campaign. By the time the actress who played his owner was on *Good Morning America,* assuring the world that Sparky was, in fact, still very much alive, I had survived the worst professional embarrassment of my career.

Barely.

And now? Now I was back in my hometown of New Orleans. Me,

my bruised ego, and the realization that if I didn't pull off this next job, I wouldn't have a career left to fix.

So I wasn't here to eat beignets and wallow in nostalgia.

I was here to work.

Not that I had much nostalgia to wallow in.

My brother and I had lost our parents when we were barely out of college, and after that, New Orleans had never really felt like home again. Not the way it used to be. No big family was waiting for me, no childhood house filled with warm memories—just the old place we grew up in, the one Jake had stayed in, and I'd left behind. Without my parents, there hadn't been much pulling me back.

At least, not until now.

Logan Richards, the rock star who was supposed to be my next client, was already fifteen minutes late. Our meeting spot? The back office of Inkwell, the bookstore-slash-coffee-shop my best friend, Sarah LeBlanc, owned and had graciously loaned me as my temporary headquarters while I was in town.

If my life were a movie, this would be the part where the childhood best friend shows up for comic relief and emotional support. Right on cue, Sarah burst through the door, balancing a tray of cookies in one hand and a coffee in the other.

"Well, well, well, Elizabeth Bailey. Look at you." She pulled me into a hug, squeezing a little too tightly. "Still in one piece. Still corporate. Still running on an unhealthy amount of caffeine?"

I huffed a laugh. I mean, she wasn't wrong.

Sarah pulled back, shoving the coffee into my hands without asking if I wanted it. "Here. It's black, like your soul."

I snorted. "You think my soul is black?"

"Well, maybe a dark espresso brown." She winked.

I took a sip, letting the warmth settle into me. Sarah stood in front of me, hands on her hips, as if taking stock. "It's good to see you." A beat. "Have you seen Jake yet?"

My stomach twisted. Of course, she'd ask about him. I forced a casual shrug. "Not yet. I'm planning to stop by as soon as I get my work under control."

Sarah raised an eyebrow. "You've been here how long?"

I exhaled, guilt creeping in. "I flew in late last night and went straight to the hotel. I'll stay at the house at night, but it's good to have a hotel room in the middle of everything. Work's been—"

"Uh-huh." She crossed her arms. "Just say you're avoiding your little brother and save us both the speech."

My stomach tightened. "I've been busy."

Sarah snorted. "You're always busy."

That was fair. I had been a workaholic since kindergarten—while other kids were learning their ABCs, I was figuring out how to recite them the fastest. Sarah never let me forget it.

"Remember field day in fourth grade?" she said, smirking. "When we were all playing tug-of-war, and you were in the corner making flashcards?"

"They were math flashcards."

She rolled her eyes. "You skipped the three-legged race to study multiplication tables."

"And yet, no one else in our class could do mental division faster than me."

She groaned. "It was *Field Day,* not the *Math Olympiad!*"

I shrugged. "Greatness doesn't take a day off."

Sarah had always been the effortlessly cool one, her brown hair pulled back in a loose braid, her smile as easy as it had been in high school. She was wiping her hands on a flour-dusted apron—she was baking again, probably those praline cookies she used to bribe teachers with during finals. Meanwhile, I was the one constantly hustling, always planning my next step.

And now, after everything that had happened, I needed to focus on fixing my PR career before it spiraled any further.

Sarah's teasing faded, and she placed a hand on my arm, her voice softer. "Hey, I'm sorry about everything that happened with Sparky. At least you're back in New Orleans, so that's something, right?"

I forced a smile. "Yeah. Except now I'm stuck fixing the image of Logan Richards, who's basically chaos in a leather jacket."

Sarah's eyes widened. "Wait. *The* Logan Richards? The rock legend?"

"The one and only," I muttered.

She let out a low whistle. "Wow. Good luck with that. I hate to say it, but this might be your biggest challenge yet."

"Gee, thanks," I deadpanned.

She grinned. "No. If anyone can pull this off, it's you. You're the best at what you do."

That earned her a half-smile.

She sighed dramatically, tossing her apron onto the counter. "I *was* planning to stick around, show your guests where everything is, maybe schmooze a little. But, alas, duty calls. I'm in the church choir, and if I don't leave now, I'll be running in mid-hymn."

"You could skip one Sunday," I suggested.

"Tempting, but I enjoy my seat in the soprano section, and skipping would be frowned upon by, you know, *God*." She grabbed her bag and pointed a stern finger at me. "It's Sunday morning, which means the place is yours. Don't burn it down."

"No promises."

Sarah rolled her eyes but grinned, gesturing around the Inkwell Café, a quirky little haven of caffeine and literature that had somehow become an institution in Mid-City New Orleans. Then she was gone, leaving me with the scent of warm pralines, too much caffeine, and the sinking realization that I was officially on my own.

I tried to breathe through my irritation at how late Logan and his manager were, but it was no use. I could be in New York right now, rebuilding my career, instead of waiting around for some rock star who had no respect for other people's time.

Across the room, I saw a book display titled *How to Keep Your Cool When Everyone Around You Is an Idiot*. I considered borrowing it.

I checked my phone. Twenty minutes late. Fantastic.

I let out a slow breath, pacing the empty room before forcing myself to stop and pretend to browse the bookshelves. If I kept myself busy, maybe I wouldn't feel like I was wasting my time.

Thirty minutes late.

I clenched my jaw, shoving my phone back into my pocket. If Logan Richards wanted to waste my time, I wasn't about to sit here twiddling my thumbs. I had some papers to work on in my car. I might as well be productive.

But this wasn't just about my time. It wasn't just about my patience.

This was my career—my reputation—my entire future on the line.

I had fought hard for this job, convinced my boss I could handle it, despite the Sparky disaster. I was supposed to be the one who could fix the unfixable, the one who could turn a PR disaster into gold. But I was learning that Logan wasn't just a disaster—he was a Category 5 hurricane barreling toward self-destruction. And if I didn't clean up his mess, if I couldn't turn his downward spiral into a redemption story, I wouldn't walk away with a failed campaign. I'd walk away without a career.

Because no one wanted a PR rep who couldn't control her client.

And right now? Logan Richards was out of control.

Something had happened in the last year. Everyone knew it. His music had always had that raw, reckless edge, but this was different. This wasn't just a rock star partying too hard or a celebrity making tabloid headlines. This was a man falling apart in real-time. A canceled tour. No-shows at major events. Paparazzi shots of him looking hollow-eyed and distant, spiraling into something that even his most die-hard fans couldn't ignore.

And there I was, expected to patch him back together.

I pressed my fingers against my temples, inhaling deeply before exhaling through my nose.

As if that wasn't enough, there was the looming shadow of his father.

That was the thing about Logan Richards—he wasn't just famous. He was legacy famous. His father wasn't some washed-up rock star from the '80s trying to relive his glory days. He was a legendary, Beatles-level rock god, his name recognized in every household. And yet, he'd seemingly disappeared. The industry hadn't heard from him in years, and I suspect that Logan, despite every attempt to carve out his place in the music world, was still buried under the weight of his last name.

That's why he was here in New Orleans.

Instead of riding out his self-destruction under the relentless glare of Los Angeles or New York, where every mistake was splashed across gossip sites within minutes, he had come to New Orleans, a city that lets its ghosts keep their secrets. A place where fame didn't matter as much, where people cared more about the music than the spectacle. If there was ever a time for him to disappear long enough to get his act together—or at least make it look like he had—this was it.

This was the moment to rehab his image.

If he didn't screw it up first.

I grabbed my half-empty coffee cup and the stack of papers I'd been scribbling on, balancing them against my phone as I pushed open the door, stepped onto the sidewalk, and slammed straight into what appeared to be a homeless man loitering outside in a hoodie and sunglasses.

Two voices warred in my head.

The New Orleans part of me: *Oh, bless his heart, let's get him a cup of coffee and some change.*

The New York part of me: *Absolutely not. You do not have time for this. Move him or move through him.*

New York won. "The store's closed. You can't hang out right here." I shifted my coffee and folder before they could spill their contents all over me.

The guy didn't budge. Just stood there, hood up, sunglasses on, hands shoved in his pockets. I tried to shield my eyes from the brutal sun.

His voice was smooth, low, and vaguely amused. "Oh, yeah?"

I exhaled sharply. "Yeah."

He tilted his head, unimpressed. "Seems like you made that rule up."

I scowled, still not looking directly at him as I fumbled with the folder. "Look, I don't have time for this. Could you please move?"

"You're kinda bossy, huh?"

"And you're kinda standing in my way."

His mouth twitched. "You always this pleasant, or is today special?"

I let out a humorless laugh. "You always this difficult?"

"You tell me." His smirk was audible, but between the sunglasses, the hoodie, and the sun blinding me, I still couldn't get a good look at him.

I rolled my eyes and stepped to the side, just as he moved the same way.

We both stopped and shifted again, resulting in another awkward mirror move.

"Oh for—" I stepped past him, and somehow, my foot clipped his, or his clipped mine, and the next thing I knew, I was crashing into him, my folder exploding in a storm of papers.

"Unbelievable," I muttered, dropping to my knees to gather the mess.

He let out a dramatic sigh and crouched down, too. "You know, if you were in less of a rush to boss people around, this wouldn't have happened."

I shot him a glare, still not seeing his face through the sun's glare and his dark lenses. "And if you had the common decency to move, this wouldn't have happened."

He handed me a paper, smirking. "Wow. You're all sunshine and rainbows."

I snatched it from him. "Wow. You're all manners and basic human decency."

He let out a low chuckle and passed me another page. "Do you always greet people with this much hostility?"

"Only when they make me trip, block my path, and generally exist in an inconvenient way."

His smirk widened. "You should try smiling. Might be good for your blood pressure."

I narrowed my eyes, still only catching glimpses of his face in the harsh sunlight. "You should try walking in a straight line. Might be good for my balance."

He handed me the last sheet, shaking his head. "Here are your papers. You know, most people would just say 'thank you.'"

I huffed. "Most people wouldn't need me to dodge around them like an obstacle course."

Before he could fire back, a third voice cut through the air.

"There you are, Logan! I parked the car. And you must be Elizabeth Bailey, PR person extraordinaire."

I froze. The voice belonged to an older man with movie-star confidence and just enough salt sprinkled in his dark hair to suggest power, charm, and a whole Rolodex of Hollywood clients.

But my focus snapped back to the much younger man standing in front of me, the one I'd mistaken for a homeless person and just snapped at, the one who'd blocked the sidewalk.

My eyes adjusted to the sun, and like a camera lens coming into focus, everything clicked.

Logan Richards.

The client I was supposed to fix.

The reason I was back in New Orleans.

He grinned, pushing his sunglasses down just enough to meet my stare. His brown hair was long enough to fall into his eyes and brush just past his ears. Sharp cheekbones, an angular jaw, and a lean, almost restless energy gave him the look of someone who lived in the moment, untethered by rules or routine.

His eyes were a deep, soulful brown that begged you to get lost in them.

And judging by his smirk, he was already enjoying how much he was getting under my skin.

Well, this was off to a great start.

# 2

## LOGAN

I SHOULD HAVE STAYED in bed.

Instead, I was here, standing in some too-cozy, too-quirky bookstore about to be lectured by my manager and some PR robot in heels about how I was ruining my career.

Fantastic.

I shoved my sunglasses up into my hair and rubbed a hand over my face. I didn't ask for this meeting. I didn't ask for any of this. But my manager, Mick Hayes, had all but dragged me here, muttering something about damage control and how my label was "this close" to dropping me.

"Finally," Mick sighed, striding into the empty shop. "Sorry, we're late." Mick was tall, broad-shouldered, with salt-and-pepper hair cut sharp around his jaw and a five o'clock shadow that somehow made him look both distinguished and dangerous. His shirt was crisp, his watch expensive, and he moved with the confidence of a man who had brokered deals in boardrooms, back alleys, and Beverly Hills brunch spots.

The PR woman checked the time on her phone before looking up, her expression smooth, her voice effortlessly composed. "No worries. I know how unpredictable schedules can be."

I almost laughed. This was not the same woman who had practically snarled at me outside.

Now she was the picture of charm and restraint, all crisp professionalism and carefully measured smiles.

Unbelievable. If she hadn't nearly stabbed me with her glare over some scattered papers, I might've bought it.

I should have let it go. But something about the way she narrowed her eyes at me got under my skin. Like she was judging me, like I was a problem she had to fix.

"I overslept," I said flatly. "Not that it's any of your business, but I was up late doing *very important things*."

Her expression didn't change. "Drinking?"

"Living." I flashed a grin.

She sat down and motioned for Mick and me to sit down as well. She folded her hands neatly on the table, offering a smooth, diplomatic smile. "I appreciate you both taking the time to meet."

"Oh yeah," I deadpanned. "Can't think of a better way to spend my day."

Mick kicked me under the table so hard that I nearly yelped.

If the sarcasm bothered her, she didn't show it. Instead, she nodded, as if I'd confirmed something she already knew, and got straight to business.

"Alright, let's talk about where things stand. Your label is concerned. Your last few press interviews didn't go well. The tabloids are running with every negative headline they can find, and there's serious talk of dropping you completely." She paused, making sure I was listening before adding, "We need to take control of the narrative before it's too late."

I leaned back in my chair, stretching my arms behind my head. "I don't see the problem."

Elizabeth blinked. "You don't see a problem with your label wanting to drop you?"

I shrugged. "They're not going to drop me. I'm in New Orleans recording my latest album. That's what matters. Who cares what the tabloids say?"

She tilted her head, studying me. "You don't see a problem with getting into a shouting match with a journalist last week?"

"Nope. He asked a stupid question."

"What about the video of you climbing a hotel balcony barefoot?"

I coughed. "That's not a big deal. I made it back inside, didn't I?"

She arched a brow. "And the fact that you may or may not have stolen a golf cart from a country club?"

I frowned. "Okay, first of all, I *borrowed* it. And second, they got it back."

Her lips pressed together like she was trying very hard not to react. "It was found in a fountain."

"Details."

Mick groaned and rubbed his temples. "This is what I'm dealing with, Elizabeth."

She exhaled slowly, like she was recalibrating, then she leveled me with a look so calm, so matter-of-fact, that it cut straight through my usual defenses.

"Logan, you don't just have an image problem. You're making yourself irrelevant."

I scoffed. "Irrelevant?"

She nodded. "Your label isn't just worried about bad press. They're worried that people are getting tired of you. The reckless rock star thing? The unpredictable antics? It's been done. And if your music isn't the story, then what are you?"

Silence settled between us.

That stung more than I wanted to admit.

I sighed. "Right. And what genius PR stunt are we pulling this time? Are you going to make me cry on cue? Give some heartfelt apology about how I've 'grown as a person'?"

Mick snorted. "Well, I was going to suggest a fake marriage."

I barked out a laugh. "Oh yeah, that's a great idea. What, you want me to find some sweet, wholesome girl next door and pretend I've been in love this whole time?"

Mick grinned. "Exactly."

He and I both laughed because, obviously, that was ridiculous.

But Elizabeth didn't laugh. She didn't even smile. Instead, she tilted her head slightly, eyes sharpening like a shark catching the scent of blood. "A fake marriage would never work."

"Exactly," I said, relieved that, for once, we agreed on something.

She continued, "If you suddenly showed up married, it would feel impulsive, chaotic—exactly the opposite of what we need. Yes, marriage is a commitment, and commitment is good, but doing it out of nowhere? That screams Vegas and a bad hangover."

I smirked. "I mean, that does sound like something I'd do."

She ignored that. "We have to be careful. If this plan backfires, it won't make you look stable—it'll make you look even *more* reckless."

I nodded. "Right. So glad we're on the same page."

"Which is why a fake marriage won't work, but a fake relationship makes much more sense."

*Wait, what?*

I blinked. "Oh, no way."

She didn't even pause. "It'll work. It might be the only thing that *will* work."

I turned to her, baffled. "Are you serious?"

She shrugged, perfectly calm. Too calm. Like she'd already done the mental math and decided this was the most efficient way to fix my life. "A well-executed staged relationship would shift the narrative. If the public sees you with someone stable and respected, it could help reset your image. Give them something else to talk about besides... well, you."

I let out a short laugh, shaking my head. "Oh, so we're just selling me off to the highest bidder now?"

"Not at all," she said smoothly, eyes steady. "You'd be getting something out of it, too."

And that's when I realized that she wasn't just thinking about this in theory. She'd already decided.

"There has to be a better way," I said. I doubted that anyone would even believe it.

It had been years since I'd even attempted anything resembling a real relationship. Had I ever? Casual was easy—no expectations, no attachments, no fallout. Women liked the idea of me: the rock star, the bad boy, the guy their friends would freak out over. And for a while, that was fine. I liked the attention, the thrill of it. The rush of knowing I could walk into any room and have someone's full, undivided admiration before I even spoke a word.

Because I wasn't just famous, I was the whole package.

The face, the voice, and the confidence that made people stop and pay attention. The sharp jawline that looked good in magazine spreads. The charm that had gotten me out of more trouble than I deserved.

And yet, here I was.

I used to care about the music, the fans, the rush of it all. But after my dad got sick, something in me just... shut off. The fight, the drive, the part of me that used to care all faded, like a song I couldn't hear anymore.

In the past year, I'd tested just how much I could screw up before someone finally pulled the plug on me entirely. And now? The industry had caught up. The label was fed up with me. My sponsorships? Gone. My tour? A disaster. And my fanbase? Even the most loyal ones were starting to waver, beginning to wonder if maybe I wasn't worth the trouble anymore.

That was what really stung.

Because it wasn't only about the money. It wasn't about selling out stadiums or having my name in lights.

It was about the music.

And if I didn't fix this, I wouldn't get to play anymore.

No more recording contracts, no more headlining tours, no more standing in front of a crowd and feeling that electric pulse of thousands of people singing my lyrics back to me.

And that? That scared me.

I didn't know who I was without it.

Elizabeth exhaled, straightening in her chair like she was preparing for battle. "Alright, let's go through other options." She started counting off on her fingers. "You could lead a music workshop for high school students."

"Sounds fun. Do they mind if I curse?"

Elizabeth squinted. "Yes."

I smiled. "Well, that's gonna be a problem. What's next?"

Elizabeth was undeterred. "Okay, what about something health-focused? A meditation retreat? Self-reflection is great PR."

I shook my head. "Pass. I don't meditate or self-reflect."

"A fitness partnership?" Elizabeth suggested. "People love a good transformation story."

Nope. "I refuse to let the internet watch me struggle through a hundred push-ups. Next."

Elizabeth nodded slowly. "You could partner with a literacy foundation, and maybe help with a reading campaign."

"Like, reading to kids?"

"That's right," she said.

"You do realize my last album had a song called 'Whiskey & Regrets,' right?"

Mick broke in then. "Yeah, let's not put him in a room full of impressionable young minds. Moving on."

Elizabeth sighed, then leaned back in her chair. "At this point, a staged relationship would be the fastest way to turn things around."

I snorted. "You're serious about this?"

"It's the only strategy that checks all the boxes: it stabilizes your image, it gives people something positive to focus on, and it makes you seem reliable."

Reliable. Right. Because that's what people wanted from me? A *dependable* rock star? Someone predictable, polished, and packaged for mass consumption?

I let out a short laugh. "Oh, right, because nothing screams 'stable' like faking a whole relationship. Mick, help me out here."

Mick cleared his throat. "I think Elizabeth is on to something. And she *is* the best in the business."

I glared at my manager. *Traitor.*

Elizabeth sat forward in the chair. "The public loves a redemption arc. A well-executed relationship could make people see you as someone they want to root for, not just another rock star spiraling out."

I stared at her. "So you're saying I need a girlfriend to make me less of a disaster?"

"Basically."

The idea of playing pretend, of pasting on a smile while some carefully chosen woman clung to my arm, was enough to make my skin crawl. I'd spent too much of my life feeling like a prop in other people's narratives. I shook my head, pushing back from the table. "Not happening."

Mick sighed. "We'll put a pin in it, but think about it, Logan. It might work."

I stormed out without another word.

But before I reached the door, I looked back at Elizabeth.

Her brown hair was twisted into a tight, no-nonsense bun. Her cheekbones were sharp, and her gaze was so cool it made me shiver.

She was controlling. Uptight. The exact kind of person I didn't need in my life. I'd had enough of people thinking they knew what was best for me. I needed space to breathe, not someone trying to run my life like a board meeting.

I walked outside, but I didn't know where the car was, so I waited for Mick. The whole meeting had been a joke, a waste of time, and now here I was, standing outside like I needed to cool off.

He came out a few minutes later. I shook my head. "She's unbelievable," I muttered. "Thinks she's got all the answers. Like she's gonna walk in here and clean up my life when she can't even handle her own."

Mick exhaled, but I wasn't finished. The words kept rolling out, the anger behind them hotter than the coffee cooling in my hands.

Because the worst part? I knew she wasn't wrong. I wasn't invincible. Not anymore.

I'd spent the last year pretending I was, daring the industry to cut me loose, to prove that I wasn't worth the trouble. And one by one, they had. The label. The sponsors. The people who used to fight for me. They'd all moved on.

I should have seen it coming. Shoot, I did see it coming.

But knowing something and being ready to fix it were two different things. And maybe that's why this whole thing made me so angry. Because I knew I needed to make a change. I knew I couldn't keep going like this. But not this way. Not with some PR handler barking orders, shoving me into a fake relationship like that was gonna fix everything.

I ran a hand over my jaw, forcing a humorless laugh. "You know Elizabeth must have messed up. Badly. You don't get kicked out of New York City and exiled to New Orleans unless you're in trouble." I took a slow sip of coffee, shaking my head. "It's pathetic. She's out here, acting like she's in control, when we both know she's one mistake away from getting tossed out of the industry for good. It's pathetic."

The words sounded cruel, even to me, but I didn't take them back. Because if I admitted she was one step away from losing everything... I'd have to admit that I was, too.

Mick shifted uncomfortably, rubbing his jaw. "Logan—"
*Click. Click. Click.*

I turned in time to see Elizabeth standing in the doorway, her silhouette framed by the dim yellow light spilling from inside.

Her arms were crossed, her face unreadable.

And yet, something about the way she stood there made my stomach tighten.

She took a step forward, her voice perfectly even. "You know what's pathetic?"

I clenched my jaw, waiting.

She tilted her head slightly, eyes locked on mine. "You. You think you're calling me out? That you're the first person to try to take me down?" She let out a soft, almost amused breath. "You're not even the first *this week.*"

I rolled my eyes, but something in my chest burned.

She stepped closer, her heels clicking deliberately against the pavement. "You say I'm horrible at my job, but here's the thing. You need me." Her gaze flicked over me, unimpressed.

I clenched my jaw, but she wasn't finished.

"You can't fix yourself, so you take shots at the person trying to help you. And why?" She gave a slow, knowing smile. "Because deep down, you know I'm right."

My chest tightened.

I took a step closer, my voice dropping. "You don't know a thing about me."

Her smile didn't waver. "I know enough." With the kind of smile that could carve through a man's gut, she turned and walked back inside, leaving me standing there in the thick, humid air.

The door clicked shut behind her.

The air around me felt quieter. Heavier.

Mick let out a long exhale, shaking his head. "She got you good."

I scoffed, lifting the coffee cup to my lips. "Please."

And yet, as I stared at the closed door, her words kept replaying in my head. *Because deep down, you know I'm right.*

I muttered a curse under my breath and threw the rest of my coffee into the gutter.

It was cold anyway.

# 3

## ELIZABETH

An hour later, I had finally calmed down enough to make the call.

There was no way I could work with Logan Richards.

He was impossible. Arrogant. Self-destructive in an infuriating way. He was the kind of man who set fire to his career and laughed while it burned. And I was supposed to fix that? To make him *likable*? It wasn't happening.

It was apparent why he was the way he was. When you grow up as the son of Ryder Richards, doors open without you even touching the handle. His father was the legendary frontman of Midnight Saints, a man practically canonized in rock history. So, Logan was terrifically talented, but he had also coasted on his last name his whole life. Fame had been his inheritance. And the consequences? Those had never stuck to someone like him.

I was trying to make that case to Vanessa Sheehan, the PR maven famous for salvaging the reputations of people no one else would touch. She was a legend in the industry—sharp, fearless, and always three steps ahead. Working under her had been like earning a master class in public image and crisis management, and everything I knew, I owed to her.

And PR? It was the perfect career for someone like me, who

needed control as much as she needed oxygen. Spin, strategy, narrative. I could anticipate problems before they happened, find solutions before the client even knew they were spiraling. While other people panicked, I planned. I took chaos and made it look polished. Controlled. Clean.

I loved the control. I loved being the one behind the curtain, pulling the strings, deciding what got said, when, and by whom. In PR, perception was reality, and I was responsible for shaping that perception. I wrote the statements. I crafted the talking points. I instructed executives on what to wear, what to post, and what to avoid. I chose which reporters got the story, how it was framed, and how much they were allowed to know. I could steer a scandal into a comeback or bury a misstep before it had a chance to gain traction.

And I was good at it.

That may be why Vanessa had taken a chance on me in the first place. It had not always been fun working for her—heck, most days it was like trying to survive psychological warfare—but she was the best. And being chosen by the best meant something, especially to a control-freak like me.

I paced the tiny courtyard behind my hotel, my phone pressed so hard against my ear that I was surprised I hadn't cracked the screen. Vanessa's clipped, icy voice came through on the other end, sharp as ever.

"Excuses, excuses, excuses. You've had *one* meeting, and suddenly, he's a lost cause? Please. I've handled clients who set hotel rooms on fire, athletes who got arrested just before the big game, and movie stars who leaked their own scandals for attention. Logan Richards is another overgrown man-child who thinks rules don't apply to him."

I pinched the bridge of my nose. "Vanessa, listen—"

"No. *You* listen. I didn't send you to New Orleans to tell me why it won't work. I sent you to *make* it work. So, I don't care if he laughed in your face, rolled his eyes, or did a tap dance on the conference table. Figure it out."

I gritted my teeth. "He doesn't care. He's not interested in fixing his image."

"Then make him interested. Find out what makes him tick, what he's afraid of, what he *wants*, and use it. That's what you do. Or have you forgotten?"

Her words hit like a slap. I squeezed my eyes shut, inhaling deeply before exhaling through my teeth.

"That's what I thought," Vanessa said. "Now, stop whining and start working."

"My point is, he's not going to do it. My fake relationship idea? He thinks it's ridiculous."

Vanessa exhaled, long and unimpressed. "And?"

"And?" I repeated, incredulous. "It's not going to work. If he won't even entertain the idea, how am I supposed to sell it?"

"That's your job, Elizabeth. You make it work."

"I can't make someone do something they refuse to do."

"Really?" Vanessa's tone turned smug. "Do you remember when Jesse Carter swore he was never going to go public with anyone after his divorce? And yet, two months later, he was on a yacht in Saint-Tropez, 'accidentally' photographed with a stunning supermodel."

I gritted my teeth, barely believing what I was hearing. "Logan Richards is not Jesse Carter."

"No, he's worse, which is why you need to be better. Find an angle. Find a reason. Make it work."

"He doesn't care, Vanessa," I said, my frustration boiling over. "About his career, about his reputation, about any of it."

Her voice was quiet, and I knew what she was going to say before she said it.

"Was I wrong to let you keep your job after the Sparky debacle?" She went there.

My stomach clenched, but I forced my voice to stay steady. "No."

"Good." Her tone was razor-sharp, cutting through whatever fight I had left. "Because let's not forget that I was the only one who took a chance on you after that mess. No one else would touch you. Do you have any idea how much damage control I had to do to keep your name off the ban list?"

I swallowed hard. Of course, I knew. I'd lived it.

She continued, "You say Logan Richards doesn't care about his career and his reputation. Then make him care. Find the right pressure point and apply pressure. If anyone can do it, it's you."

I let out a slow breath, my grip tightening on the phone. "And if I can't?"

"Then don't bother coming back to New York."

The line went dead before I could respond. I stared at the phone, half-wishing it would burst into flames in my hand.

"Great," I muttered, collapsing into one of the iron chairs in the courtyard. "No pressure."

Somewhere in the distance, jazz drifted over the rooftops, the only reminder that I was still in New Orleans. Vanessa was relentless, and I had to find a way to convince Logan to participate in this fake relationship.

I didn't have a choice.

I pulled out my phone, scrolling until I found Mick's number.

If we were going to scrub Logan's reputation, I needed to get his manager on board.

# 4

## LOGAN

MICK GOT me back here with a single sentence: *"Work with her, or I'm done managing you."*

My blood ran cold.

Mick had been with me from the start. He was the only person in this industry I trusted. He'd looked out for me when no one else did. When even my father never did.

And now, he was threatening to walk away.

So eighteen hours later, there I was, slouched in a chair at that same coffee shop, barely keeping my irritation in check. At the same time, Elizabeth Bailey—the most infuriating person I'd ever met—stood at the head of the room, flipping through her paperwork like she was unveiling a cure for cancer.

The woman had spreadsheets. So many spreadsheets. Color-coded, alphabetized, and packed into folders.

"Here are the potential candidates for the relationship," she said, her tone as steady as a metronome.

"Candidates?" I interrupted, raising an eyebrow.

She didn't look at me, just slid a stack of glossy headshots across the table.

"For your image-enhancement alliance—"

"My *what*?"

She sighed, annoyed. "Your fake relationship, Logan. I've already spoken with their representatives. These are women with clean reputations, broad appeal, and good chemistry with your brand."

I picked up the stack, flipping through the headshots. They were all polished, perfect, with the kind of fake smiles you see on magazine covers. Starlets, influencers, and even an Olympic gold medalist. Each photo had notes attached: "Pros" and "Cons."

I glanced at the first sheet. The woman in the picture was blonde, probably about twenty-five, with teeth so white they could blind someone.

**Pros:** Respected actress, wholesome public image, ties to several charitable organizations.

**Cons:** Dated another rock star last year; limited social media presence.

I handed the sheet to Mick, who was sitting next to me. "Dated a rock star last year? She's got experience with your kind, Logan. I see why that's listed as a 'con.'"

I groaned. "How do I make this decision?"

Elizabeth didn't flinch. "We have metrics, Logan. Chemistry ratings. Audience-alignment percentages..."

The following photograph was of a lovely brunette with long, wavy hair. Gorgeous, but gave me kindergarten-teacher vibes. I handed the next headshot to Mick. He held it up, looking amused. "Ooh, reality-show veteran. Pros: 'viral potential.' Cons: also 'viral potential.'" He laughed.

Elizabeth didn't blink. "She's been on *The Bachelor*. I would move to the next candidate."

Next headshot: a brunette with intense eyes and a note: "*known for charity work, faint social conscience.*" I snorted.

"Faint social conscience?" Mick echoed. "Does that mean she saves kittens... once a year?"

I kept flipping until I caught something familiar. I froze.

"Oh no." Elizabeth lunged for the sheet. "That's not for your eyes."

I grabbed the page before she could stop me.

**Logan Richards – Pros:** Charismatic, large fanbase, substantial streaming numbers, musical genius from a famous family.

**Logan Richards – Cons:** Known for erratic behavior, past scandals, challenging to work with, self-sabotaging, and arrogant. Craves attention but hates accountability. Unable to sustain professional relationships. Doesn't seem to care about his career or reputation. Bottom line: a PR nightmare.

My jaw tightened. So, my cons outweighed my pros.

By quite a bit.

"Difficult to work with?" I repeated, holding up the paper.

Elizabeth finally looked at me, her gaze cool and unflinching. "Am I wrong?"

I tossed the paper onto the table, letting it slide across the surface. "You think pairing me up with some Barbie doll is going to fix everything, make the world forget every headline about me?"

She straightened her spine. "I think it's a start. If you want to regain control of your career, you need to start shaping the narrative. And this is how we do it. Don't you care about your family's legacy?"

My family's legacy.

The words hit like a punch to the gut. My chair scraped against the floor as I shot to my feet before I even realized what I was doing. "Control the narrative?" My voice came out sharp, bitter. "You sound like *him*."

"Logan," Mick said, warningly.

Elizabeth blinked, tilting her head slightly. "I sound like him? I... I don't know what that means."

Of course, she didn't. No one ever did.

No one understood what it was like to be Ryder Richards' son. To have your last name mean something before you even knew who you were. To have the world expect you to be brilliant, wild, magnetic, and to punish you when you weren't. To have your father be a legend to everyone but you. The anger bubbled up before I could stop it. "This whole idea is ridiculous. You want to put me in a box, slap a label on me, and sell me like I'm some PR product. Newsflash, sweetheart: I'm not for sale."

She flinched, just slightly, but enough that I caught it. "You don't want to do this? Fine. Go ahead and keep making headlines for all the wrong reasons. See how long your label sticks around."

The silence stretched, tense and uncomfortable, until Mick cleared his throat.

"Logan," he said again, his tone icy.

I didn't answer. I grabbed the stack of headshots and stalked out of the room, my frustration boiling over. Outside, the heat wrapped around me like a suffocating blanket.

I pulled my phone from my pocket, thumb hovering over Mick's number.

I'd tell him I wasn't doing this, that I didn't need him. That he could go ahead and walk away.

But I didn't call. Because I knew the second I heard his voice, I'd cave.

He meant it. He was done. And without him? Without Mick?

I was alone.

My stomach twisted. I exhaled sharply, turned on my heel, and marched back inside. Elizabeth and Mick didn't look surprised when I walked in. I dropped into the chair, rolling my shoulders like this wasn't a surrender.

"Fine," I said flatly. "Let's pick my girlfriend."

# 5

## ELIZABETH

THERE WE WERE: on a fake date at Lakeview Harbor.

I'd never done this with a client before, but something told me Logan needed it. He was a live wire who, to my knowledge, had never once been seen on a calm, normal date. That gap in his "experience portfolio" made me nervous. So, we were on a date.

Not that Logan knew that.

Lakeview Harbor wasn't the fanciest spot in New Orleans, but it was quiet, relaxed, and best of all, their hamburgers were legendary. Precisely the kind of place where I could trick Logan into practicing being charming without the paparazzi breathing down our necks.

After countless headshots and an exhausting number of pros-and-cons lists, Logan, Mick, and I finally landed on Sophie Hartwell as his fake girlfriend. She was a starlet on the rise, fresh off her breakout role in a wholesome, feel-good Netflix hit called *The Sweet Spot* that had made her a household name overnight. With her honey-blonde waves, all-American dimples, and wide-eyed charm, she had the perfect balance of Midwestern sweetness and budding Hollywood glamour.

I was sitting in the chair opposite Logan. "Sophie's team's thrilled with this arrangement. I mean, of course, they are. Sophie's on the cusp of real fame but isn't quite a superstar yet. So, dating an international rock god and certified bad boy will catapult her even farther into the public eye. A carefully crafted romance with you gives her an instant edge, an air of intrigue, without tarnishing her wholesome, girl-next-door image."

"Oh, goody for me," he said.

"It *is* good for you," I pressed. "She's got zero scandal. No messy exes. Actually, we couldn't find any exes at all. First time I've seen that. A spotless reputation. That means no headlines to compete with, no past drama to distract from your redemption arc. I did pretty well, if I do say so myself."

He leaned back, steepling his fingers. "Tell me again how this helps me?"

"First, it's the perfect fodder for rebranding. You'll be known as the bad boy who turned it around for love. And that opens up every other door that's currently closing on you. Your label will be relieved that love has returned you to respectability. And your fans? Everyone loves a reformed rock star, and when it's romance that reformed him... They'll *eat this up*."

Logan didn't react. This guy was raised on the kind of privilege that let him coast through life without effort. The type who rolled their eyes at rules and then expected someone else to pick up the pieces when everything inevitably exploded.

Luckily, I knew how to handle people like that: Tough love. "I think Sophie Hartwell will be perfect for you."

Logan shifted in his seat. "Perfect for me?"

"Yes." I forced my voice to stay light. "Sweet. Charming. A national treasure. The exact opposite of your entire public persona. She's not your type, but she's perfect."

That got his attention. His eyes flashed, like he was flirting with me. He leaned in, slow and deliberate: "My type?"

I ignored the way my stomach dipped. "Oh, you know. Women who make bad decisions. All your exes with trust funds and daddy issues."

"Wow. Tell me how you really feel."

I shrugged. "Just saying, if I ran the numbers, there'd be a strong correlation between your past relationships and women who only date musicians because their therapist told them not to."

Logan let out a short laugh, shaking his head. "And yet, here you are, setting me up with America's sweetheart."

I sighed dramatically. "I think it'll be good for you to date an actual functioning adult for once. Now, practice with me. Pretend I'm Sophie. Ask what looks good to me on the menu."

He stared at me, utterly baffled. "Why would I do that?"

I kept my tone flat, as if I were clarifying instructions in a training manual. "Just do it."

"Uh, what looks good to you?"

"I love the steak frites here. They're crispy, buttery, and irresistible." I waited for him to say something. When he didn't, I continued my act. "Now tell me that you loved *The Sweet Spot*. That I was so convincing in it."

"You were... convincing in it?" He cocked his head. "You were *in* it?"

"Of *course* I wasn't in it. Sophie was."

He blinked. "Wait—are we on a *fake date* to prepare me for *fake dating* Sophie?"

*He was so frustrating in the way that he had to fight me at every turn.* I narrowed my eyes. "You're about to enter a three-month PR relationship, and based on your past dating history, I'd say you could use some pointers."

"I don't need pointers."

I gave him a look. "You absolutely do."

He smirked. "I think I can handle a date."

I arched an eyebrow. "Can you, though?"

Logan sighed dramatically. "Fine. Teach me, oh wise one. How does one properly pretend to be smitten with a Hollywood sweetheart?"

I ignored his sarcasm.

"Ask questions. Show interest. Make her feel like the most fascinating person in the world."

Logan snorted. "She's an actress. She already thinks that."

I leveled him with a look. "Logan."

He sighed. "Fine. Ask questions. Got it."

"Well... then ask me something about myself."

Logan looked up and tilted his head. "So, tell me, is it true that you killed Sparky, America's favorite dog?"

"Very funny." I set my glass of water down. "You know that I didn't kill Sparky. Sparky's very much alive. It was a press release that wasn't supposed to go out."

Logan let out a low whistle. "That's... *rough*. No pun intended."

I shot him a look. "Thanks for that."

"I mean, that press release was *paws-itively* disastrous."

I inhaled sharply through my nose. *Keep it together, Bailey.* "I need you to be serious. Okay, let's talk strategy."

Logan squinted. "What strategy?"

"Date strategy. You should bring Sophie something before every date."

"Okay, you realize that these are fake dates, right?"

"Even for a fake date, you can't show up empty-handed."

Logan frowned. "Like, what should I bring? A stuffed animal with a giant heart?"

I sighed. "Nothing over the top. Something small. Something that makes it look like you thought about her before you showed up. Or pick a flower and present it to her."

He gave me a flat look. "I don't do flowers."

Of course he didn't.

I exhaled, resisting the urge to rub my temples. Logan Richards was the most infuriating client I'd ever had.

He hated being managed and hated being told what to do. Every look, every dismissive shrug, every smirk screamed, *You can't control me.* But control was what I did best. It was what made me good at my job. I needed to control the message, the timing, the narrative... and yes, the client.

And I always won.

Logan Richards might fight me every step of the way, but in the end, I would get what I needed from him—his cooperation, his compliance, his face on the cover of a magazine looking like a reformed golden boy. Because I had no choice. If I couldn't pull this off, if I couldn't make him cooperative and redeemable, then I could kiss my career goodbye.

No one would want a publicist who couldn't even handle a simple fake relationship rollout.

# 6

# LOGAN

If Elizabeth Bailey could've skewered me with her fork instead of stabbing at her steak, she absolutely would have.

Apparently, I was on a fake date with her—practice for my upcoming "real" fake date with Sophie Hartwell—and I couldn't resist getting under her skin.

It served her right for trying to tell me how to behave, like when she imparted this little nugget: "Try not to make the date about you. Ask questions. Be present. And maybe don't lead with your platinum record count."

I raised an eyebrow. "What if it comes up naturally?"

"It won't."

I cleared my throat and leaned in, mocking sincerity. Let's see how she likes this for small talk: "Wow, Sophie...you've had so much plastic surgery, I literally don't recognize you. It's like you're a whole new person."

Elizabeth glared. I could practically feel the anger radiating off her. She flashed the world's most insincere grin at me. "Ha, ha, ha. But seriously, I hope you don't actually say that to Sophie."

Did she think I had no filter? "Relax. I'm not going to bring up plastic surgery. I'm not *completely* unhinged."

She rolled her eyes and took a slow, theatrical sip of her drink. "Great. Then how about you try this: tell me how amazing this place is and offer me a bite of your food."

I looked down at my massive burger, already mostly devoured. "This bacon-cheddar masterpiece is the stuff of legends. You want a bite?"

She gave me a look like I'd just offered her my toothbrush. "Yeah, that's gonna be a no."

I lifted a lone broccolini spear from my plate, offering it to her as if it were some grand romantic gesture. "Here. One broccolini, just for you."

Her lips stayed firm. "That's better. But, no, thank you, not right now."

I flashed a grin and waved the vegetable around like a plane. "Oh, come on... yum yum. Open the hangar, bring in the plane. Vroom, vroom."

She met my eyes with a sharp look, but there was something amused hiding underneath. "Is that your standard dating technique? Because I'm starting to think you need a whole lot more help than I thought."

I laughed in spite of myself. "My dating technique's just fine." I tipped my chin toward Elizabeth, shooting her a suggestive look.

Her breath hitched subtly, and her throat rose and fell. A flicker in her gaze, an almost imperceptible catch in her voice, and in that moment, I knew: the game was working exactly as I intended.

Before she could steady herself or deliver a killer comeback, the restaurant manager materialized, starstruck and wide-eyed. "Oh wow —Logan Richards. I saw you at Red Rocks last year. You were unreal."

I nodded politely. "Thanks, man. That was a good crowd."

The manager beamed at Elizabeth. "And are you a model or movie star or something?"

She leveled him with a calm smile. "No, this is a professional meeting—I'm far from a model or movie star."

I leaned in, voice teasing, and caught the manager's eye. "Far from, huh? I'd argue she's prettier than any model or movie star I've ever worked with."

I saw her pause mid-breath, just long enough to see the color bloom in her cheeks. My chest tightened. *Sweet.* I'd hit a nerve. I added softly, "Every time you blush like that, I want to hit rewind and watch it again."

She glowered. I kept going, charm dialed up. "Seriously, I love to make you laugh."

Her jaw clenched. "Like I said—this is a professional meeting."

I tapped the menu to catch Elizabeth's attention. "Actually...how about dessert? Maybe we could share that molten lava cake."

Her gaze snapped to the nearby manager. "We won't be sharing dessert. This is *not* a date. Do you understand?"

The manager nodded so vigorously his head might've fallen off. "Yes, ma'am."

I gave her the ole puppy dog eyes. I was enjoying the way her cheeks flushed when she was flustered. "Oh, come on. Two spoons, one cake. I'll even let you have the first bite, sweetheart."

Elizabeth's eyes ignited. She raised her voice, in case anyone was listening. "No. And we're taking separate cars to separate residences when we leave. Is that clear? To everyone?"

The manager hovered, clearly regretting showing up tonight. "Crystal."

I turned back to Elizabeth with one perfectly charming shrug. "At your decibel, I think it's clear to everyone in the restaurant."

She nodded curtly. "I'll pay the check." She pulled her card forward and added quietly, "It's on the company." The manager scurried off, relieved.

I watched him leave, then smirked and asked, "Was I charming enough?"

Elizabeth sighed. "Clearly, you know what to do on a date."

I pivoted, offering what I thought would be the smoothest move. "May I escort you to your car? Open your door. Make sure you get home safely. I want to prove that I can be a good boy."

Her lips tensed into a tight line. "No. Just don't be late tomorrow."

I clenched my teeth, swallowing the irritation. "Oh, right, I have to meet my girlfriend."

As I drove away, frustration twisted in my chest. I would show up tomorrow, but I was more certain than ever that I needed to find an exit strategy. And fast.

## 7

# ELIZABETH

Logan Richards was on the brink of meeting his new girlfriend. Unfortunately, in the meantime, he was seriously testing my patience.

The practice date last night had been a disaster. Clearly, he enjoyed pushing my buttons with Olympic precision. And now? He was sprawled in a chair across from me in the private meeting room Sarah had let me borrow at Inkwell Cafe, scrolling through his phone like a teenager bored in study hall.

"So," I said, arms crossed and tone sharp, "have you done your homework? Have you watched *The Sweet Spot* yet? You know, the show that made Sophie Hartwell a household name?"

He looked up slowly, like he'd just woken from a nap, smirk firmly in place. "Sophie who?"

I blinked. "Sophie Hartwell, the woman who will be walking through that door in two minutes. The woman you're about to pretend is the love of your life for the next three months."

He shrugged. "Doesn't ring a bell. Are you sure that's a real name? Sounds made-up."

I leaned in. "Yes, Logan. Maybe you should tattoo her name on your hand so you don't forget it in interviews."

Before he could respond, the door swung open. Sarah strolled in, humming, a plate of fresh cookies in her hands. "I thought you all might want something sweet," she said, setting it between us. "These are brown butter-sea salt with just a hint of espresso." Then, with a nod, she quietly slipped out, letting the door click shut behind her.

Logan didn't even look up. He simply pushed the plate an inch closer to me.

I inhaled sharply through my nose. This meeting was where we'd finalize everything. We'd define boundaries, draft a timeline, and ensure both parties were on the same page.

Sophie wasn't big enough to have a whole entourage flying out with her to New Orleans. Not yet, at least. So, it would just be Logan, Sophie, and me at the meeting.

And if Logan could follow directions for once in his life, we might pull this off.

His eyes were back on his phone, ignoring me. I pressed my hands flat against my lap to keep from tapping my nails against the table. Polite. Professional. Poised. That was the job. That was what I had spent years perfecting.

New Orleans Elizabeth had been all sweetness and light, full of Southern charm and easy smiles. New York Elizabeth? She had razor-sharp edges and didn't waste time being nice.

The problem? I was still both.

And right now, New York Elizabeth wanted to snatch that phone out of his hand and throw it across the room.

Luckily, before I did, the door swung open, and Sophie Hartwell swept in like she'd been bathed in golden-hour lighting.

"Sorry I'm late! I had to dodge a few paparazzi," she said, flipping her honey-blonde hair over her shoulder, and giggling as if she had said something hilarious. I could already tell that she was one of those women who laughed at everything.

She was all warmth, all effortless charm. She floated to the table, beaming at Logan first, then me, like she'd walked into a party instead of a PR crisis summit.

Logan sat up a little straighter. Just barely. If I hadn't been watching him like a hawk, I wouldn't have noticed it.

Sophie slipped into the seat next to him, her smile luminous. "I hear we're going to be madly in love."

Logan let out a short laugh, his tension from before vanishing instantly. "So they say."

I cleared my throat, adjusting the sleeve of my blazer. "Right. Let's get down to it. Sophie, as the wholesome balance to Logan's... well, Logan, you'll help rebuild his public image, smooth over the drama, and get him back on track."

Sophie nodded eagerly, giggling again. I was pretty sure I would hear that sound frequently over the next few months. Turning to Logan, she leaned in, head tilted, eyes bright. "I love it. Sounds amazing." Just her tone alone made it feel like everything was already perfect.

I studied her, watching the way she tilted her chin.

She was perfect. Too perfect. I should have been relieved that she was all in. Instead, my stomach twisted for some unknown reason.

Logan was leaning into it. Oh, he was still irritated by the whole concept, but now he was paying attention. Now he was playing along.

The chemistry between them was apparent. Easy.

That's what he needed. Someone like Sophie who could handle his chaos, someone who lived in his world, someone who craved the spotlight.

If this didn't save his career, nothing would.

# 8

## LOGAN

I'D SEEN a lot of badly-written lyrics in my life. Still, nothing prepared me for the overwritten, overanalyzed, and ridiculous fake relationship contract Elizabeth Bailey wanted me to sign.

"Third clause, subsection B: 'Monthly jointly publicized appearances at three-tiered charity events.'" Elizabeth's fingers flew across her laptop keys like she was drafting the Magna Carta instead of a PR stunt.

I slouched deeper into my chair as she scrolled. My pulse hit fast-forward. "This feels excessive."

Elizabeth didn't even glance up. "It's necessary."

Sophie, perched happily beside me, tapped a manicured finger against the table. "Okay, so to recap. The agreement is to be in a relationship for three months and attend at least six high-profile events together. All I have to do is be me, but Logan"—she peered at the contract and read from its pages—"will not, under any circumstances, ruin this with 'unfortunate choices.'"

I raised an eyebrow. "Unfortunate choices?"

Elizabeth stared me down. "Scandals."

I smirked. "Define scandal."

She sighed through her nose, her hands still flying over the keyboard. "Scandals include, but are not limited to, bar fights, arrest warrants, inappropriate tattoos, destroying hotel rooms, offensive social media activity, and any public behavior that lands you on TMZ."

Sophie trilled a laugh, tucking a strand of honey-blonde hair behind her ear. "Well, that's no fun. I feel like Logan would look great with an inappropriate tattoo."

I smiled. "Depends. What's the tattoo?"

"Something classic." She giggled. "Maybe a butterfly on your lower back."

Elizabeth didn't even look up. "No tattoos."

I pointed at her. "Noted."

Sophie beamed. "Logan and I need to be believable. We should have a signature thing. What about matching bracelets?"

Elizabeth gave a flat "No."

Sophie pouted. "Matching necklaces?"

Elizabeth flipped a page in her legal pad. "Okay, next: public interactions. We need a game plan for how we present the relationship."

I groaned, dragging a hand down my face. "You're telling me there's a rulebook on how to hold hands now?"

Elizabeth straightened. "Yes, actually."

I blinked. "That was sarcasm."

She handed me a printed document.

It was titled 'Public Interactions & The Art of Believability.'

I stared at it. Then at her. Then, back at the over-the-top document in my hands.

Sophie took a sip of her water. "I'd like to suggest incorporating 'cute couple moments' for the fans. Nothing too staged. It should feel organic. Feeding each other beignets, dancing at a jazz club, twinning outfits—"

I turned to Sophie, horrified. "Twinning outfits?"

Elizabeth didn't blink before shooting down the plan. "No."

I smirked. "You okay over there, Elizabeth? You know, you should try to relax."

She gave me a tight smile. "You should try taking something seriously."

Sophie giggled. "I think Logan cares a lot. He just has a funny way of showing it."

The contract conversation dragged on for far too long, covering everything from clauses and conditions to legalities and event schedules, and even a ridiculous segment on the appropriate duration of public eye contact.

Sophie giggled a lot. A never-ending stream of tiny, fluttery laugh bubbles clogging up the air.

Clearly, she was into this whole fake-relationship show.

I, on the other hand, felt like I was being slowly suffocated by fine print and forced enthusiasm. Like I'd agreed to fake date someone and accidentally signed up for a very tedious cult.

Across the table, Elizabeth was thriving.

To me, the whole thing felt like a prison sentence.

And Elizabeth was the warden.

I knew her type. Control freak, perfectionist, lives and dies by the rules. She was the kind of person who thrived on structure, the way I thrived on chaos.

Sophie was the one I was pretending to date. Sophie was easy. Sweet, agreeable, charming. The kind of person who didn't need me to be anything other than a photogenic accessory.

Elizabeth, on the other hand? She wanted order, responsibility, a plan.

She wanted to change me.

Just like my father did.

The thought settled heavily in my chest. The words weren't the same, but the message was. You're not enough as you are.

I rubbed a thumb along the edge of the table, pushing back the itch under my skin.

My father had spent years trying to mold me. And now here was Elizabeth Bailey, clipboard in hand, picking up where he left off.

At least he wasn't here to see this.

I forced a smirk and leaned back in my chair, stretching my arms behind my head like I didn't have a care in the world. "So, if I sign this, do I officially belong to you?"

Elizabeth didn't even look up from her laptop. "You wanted your career back. This is how you do it."

I tensed. "Yeah? And what if I don't want to be controlled?"

She sighed, looking unimpressed. "It's not about control, Logan. It's about strategy."

"Same thing," I muttered, clenching my jaw. I was done with this conversation. I shoved my chair back, standing up, even though I knew I had nowhere to go.

That was the thing. I could be as angry as I wanted, could act like this whole thing was some massive inconvenience, but at the end of the day, I wasn't the one calling the shots. Not anymore.

I needed this. I needed the carefully orchestrated PR miracle Elizabeth was trying to pull out of thin air. Without it, my career wasn't just in trouble, it was over.

So, yeah. I knew I had to do this.

Letting Elizabeth boss me around and pretending to be madly in love with Sophie Hartwell. Playing along for three months, as if my career depended on it. Because, unfortunately, it did.

I could sit here and let them script my life, telling me how to behave and deciding who I was supposed to be.

But I didn't have to like it.

I shoved the pen across the table and signed away the next three months of my life.

Done. Over. No turning back.

# 9

## ELIZABETH

When you want to save someone's reputation, show them saving puppies or babies.

I decided to go with puppies.

I'm instant proof that accidentally killing a dog can ruin your career, so it stands to reason that saving one can only help. It was textbook PR strategy—a simple, foolproof way to make Logan Richards look less like a tabloid train wreck and more like a man who could responsibly hold a leash without causing national controversy.

That's why the perfect first date for Logan and Sophie was a dog adoption day in New Orleans City Park.

I stood off to the side at the small dog park, called City Bark. My clipboard was in one hand, and I scanned the crowd for any signs of disaster. The event was carefully orchestrated. A local shelter provided the dogs, a handful of strategically invited photographers had cameras at the ready, and Sophie Hartwell was positively glowing in the late afternoon sun, already cooing at a tiny corgi.

Sophie flashed a megawatt grin as she twirled slightly, positioning herself at the perfect angle for the cameras. She giggled. "Aren't they precious?"

Logan, on the other hand, stood next to Sophie, looking as though he had just been sentenced to community service.

It was a good thing I had a direct line to his ear.

I activated my mic. "Try to look like you're enjoying yourself. Maybe even smile."

Logan didn't glance my way.

And he sure didn't smile.

I couldn't help but be annoyed. Because no matter how much I'd prepped him, no matter how many last-minute coaching sessions we'd had, I knew Logan Richards was about as easy to control as a tornado in a leather jacket.

I clicked my mic again. "Logan, tilt your body toward Sophie a little. It'll look more natural for the cameras."

Nothing.

I tried again. "Logan, put your arm on Sophie's shoulder. It tests well."

Instead of turning to Sophie and playing the part of the doting boyfriend and securing the perfect photo-op, he pulled out his phone.

I clenched my jaw. Was he seriously about to check his texts right now?

I forced my voice to stay even. "Logan, put your phone—"

And then he yanked the earpiece right out of his ear.

Ripped it out and tossed it in his pocket like it was an annoying piece of lint instead of the only thing keeping him on script.

No earpiece meant no control. No control meant my client was about to go rogue in the middle of a carefully curated PR event that was supposed to be cute, wholesome, and entirely scripted.

I launched out of my hiding spot behind the staging area, ignoring the weird looks from the photographers and volunteers as I speed-walked toward him. This was my job on the line. Logan Richards had already burned through a dozen second chances. If this didn't work, and if he managed to make adopting puppies *controversial*, then it was my reputation going up in flames right next to his.

I was halfway there when chaos hit.

A scrappy, wiry-haired mutt named Buttons, the problem child of the adoption event, came barreling out of nowhere, ears flopping wildly, leash trailing behind him like a rogue firehose.

Buttons had been the last pick, the dog nobody wanted. Not because he wasn't cute—he was all spindly legs, shaggy fur, and a face that somehow looked permanently surprised—but because he didn't follow the rules. Every other dog sat nicely, wagged politely, and did their job being adorable little PR props.

Buttons? Bolted every second he saw an opening.

Which, right now, was directly at Logan.

"Logan, move!" I shouted.

Too late.

Buttons collided full-speed with Logan's legs, tangled in his leash, and the leash wound around Logan's ankle three times in under five seconds.

Logan stumbled, windmilling his arms as he tried to catch his balance.

Sophie shrieked and leaped back onto a bench like she'd witnessed an actual crime. "Oh no, I can't run in these shoes!"

I dove for the leash.

So did Logan.

Instead of grabbing the leash, we grabbed each other.

And then we were both falling.

Somehow, I ended up flat on my back, Logan's weight pressing into me, my breath catching at the solid warmth of him.

For a second, neither of us moved.

His face was too close.

I could feel the warmth of him, his chest rising and falling against mine, his breath still uneven from the impact. His eyes locked onto mine, and it was like every nerve in my body lit up at once.

Nope. Absolutely not.

I shoved the feeling aside and immediately pushed myself up, untangling myself from him like I couldn't get away fast enough. I smoothed down my skirt, ignoring the heat still prickling at the back of my neck.

And then Buttons, still vibrating with chaotic energy, lunged at Logan and attacked his face with enthusiastic, slobbering licks.

I braced for Logan to lose it. To shove the dog away, to curse, to give me one more problem to deal with in this absolute disaster of a day.

Instead...

He laughed.

A real, unfiltered, genuine laugh. Not the snarky, bitter kind he usually wielded like a weapon, but something warm, surprised, completely unguarded.

I froze.

Logan Richards, laughing.

Not at me, not at some sarcastic joke. He actually sounded happy.

He scrubbed a hand over Buttons' wiry fur, grinning as the dog wagged his entire body in excitement. "Alright, alright, you win, little dude," he murmured, scratching behind his floppy ears.

Logan scratched behind its ears, murmuring something low under his breath that I couldn't quite catch.

My heart softened.

Against my will.

Against all logic, all sense, all previous experience with this man.

I should have been moving.

I should have been getting Sophie over here, making sure the cameras were capturing the right angles, doing my actual job.

But instead, I just stood there, watching.

Watching the way Logan's rough, calloused hands moved carefully over the dog's fur. Watching how his whole posture softened, how the tension he always carried around like armor disappeared. Watching how his smile wasn't for the cameras.

It was for the dog.

And for a second, I forgot why I was even there.

I blinked hard, shaking the cobwebs out of my head. Focus. This wasn't about Logan being sweet with a dog. This was about making sure the world saw it.

I spun on my heel, scanning the area until I spotted Sophie, who was standing off to the side, still looking vaguely horrified by the entire situation.

Fixable. Easily fixable.

I slipped into PR mode, crossing the distance in a few quick strides. "Sophie," I said, plastering on a warm, encouraging smile. "This is perfect. Get in there. Laugh. Touch his arm. Look like you're having fun."

She hesitated. "With... the dog?"

I fought the urge to groan. "With Logan. And the dog. C'mon let's go."

To her credit, Sophie recovered quickly, pasting on her most charming, girl-next-door expression as she followed me over to Logan.

She looped her arm through his, pressing against his side. To my surprise, he didn't flinch.

When the cameras snapped, he smiled.

And just like that, the moment was theirs.

The puppy, finally sensing that it had secured Logan as its new best friend, plopped itself right onto his foot, panting happily, wagging its whole body in delight.

Sophie clapped her hands. "Let's take him for a walk! How cute would that be?"

She wasn't wrong.

I tilted my head, murmuring: "If we advertise this puppy as the one you two walked, he'll get adopted in a heartbeat."

Logan froze. "What about the rest of them?"

I hesitated. "What do you mean?"

Logan gestured at the dogs that were older, scruffier, a little less picture-perfect than Buttons. "What happens to the rest of them?"

"I mean," I started carefully, "that's... kind of how it works. The cute ones get more attention, and—"

"Nope." Logan stood up, dusting off his jeans. "That's not gonna work for me."

He pulled his phone out of his pocket and started typing furiously.

I panicked. "What are you doing?"

"Using my biggest asset."

At first, I bristled, thinking he was about to flaunt some reckless stunt that would've made headlines. My mind raced through all the PR nightmares his "assets" had caused.

I looked over his shoulder to see what he was doing on his phone. He was posting to social media, not only about Buttons, but about the whole shelter. A series of photos and videos with the caption: "Let's get all these guys adopted. Who's got room for a new best friend?"

I blinked. I didn't expect this. Not from the guy who had spent the last few days mocking this entire process, acting like he was too cool to care, too above it all to play the game.

Sophie squealed, grabbing Logan's arm. "OH MY GOSH, this is perfect! Your fans are going to love this! It's such a good look for you."

But Logan wasn't listening. He wasn't smirking or rolling his eyes or making some sarcastic remark about damage control. His focus was still on Buttons, absentmindedly rubbing behind the dog's ears, like he hadn't even considered what this meant for his image.

And his fans?

They went wild. Almost instantly.

Within minutes, the internet exploded. The posts that Logan had made to social media went viral before I could even process what was happening. Likes, shares, and comments flooded in. Over the next couple of hours, New Orleans residents began to arrive at City Bark, eager to adopt and catch a glimpse of Logan and Sophie. Fans offered to sponsor adoptions. Organizations jumped in to match donations. The shelter's website crashed under the sudden wave of traffic.

The media picked it up next. Journalists, in addition to the pre-arranged photographers that my office had hired, arrived at the dog park. News outlets called the shelter, scrambling for interviews. And the best part? None of it was manufactured. This wasn't a PR stunt, with strategy and manipulation. It was just Logan being unexpected, unpredictable, kneeling in the dirt with a scrappy mutt who had chosen him.

I'd spent days believing I had him figured out as a rock star who didn't take anything seriously, a reckless bad boy who didn't think about consequences until it was too late.

But what if I'd been wrong?

What if he wasn't reckless, but just unpredictable? What if he wasn't careless, but just selective about what he cared about?

At that moment, he genuinely cared about these animals.

And for the first time, I realized that maybe Logan Richards didn't need me to make him look like a better person.

Maybe he already was one.

# 10

## LOGAN

THE FIRST DATE had been a smash hit. The photos were everywhere. Our new relationship even made *The New York Times*.

Who said hard-hitting journalism was dead?

Everyone was saying Sophie had tamed me.

Tamed. Like I was some rabid animal they found in the wild and rehabbed with a bit of positive reinforcement and a leash.

Still, the headlines were good. The internet was eating it up. And Elizabeth wanted to capitalize on the momentum.

I should have been okay with it. Fake dating Sophie Hartwell was easy. She was charming, knew how to play to the cameras, and did most of the work for me.

Date number two: making king cake.

The second we hit the sidewalk in front of the bakery, the cameras zeroed in. Flashing, clicking, the usual circus. I pasted on the smirk they all wanted, but inside, I was rolling my eyes.

Sophie, on the other hand, was thriving.

She waved to the crowd, blowing a kiss to one of the photographers, flashing the kind of smile that could power a small city. I barely had time to adjust my jacket before she looped her arm through mine, tilting her head just so, perfectly positioning us for the shot.

She was a pro.

After a few carefully staged moments of us laughing on cue and looking like the world's most photogenic couple, Elizabeth gave a subtle nod from the sidelines, and we finally moved inside. The kitchen smelled like butter and cinnamon.

Elizabeth's voice appeared in my ear, barking out her pre-date instructions. "Try to be more engaging this time," she said, barely looking up as she flipped through her notes. "Sophie said you were 'present but distant' last time."

"That's literally my entire personality."

Elizabeth shot me a sharp look from across the room.

I coughed. "Fine. What do you want me to do? Gaze into her eyes while we knead dough together? Confess my fake feelings?"

She pinched the bridge of her nose. "Make an effort. You're supposed to be having fun."

Having fun. Good luck with that.

However, Sophie was immediately in her element, giggling like mad, chatting with the bakers, flattering the head chef, and cooing over a fancy wedding cake.

I hung back, observing the chaos, while she twirled her way through the room like she was born to be there. She made sure to angle herself toward the cameras every time she sprinkled cinnamon over the dough.

And me? I was trying not to look like an idiot. But I guess I wasn't the one who needed to be worried about that because the moment I heard the panicked yelp, I knew something was about to go down.

I looked up in time to see a young baker, wide-eyed, sweating, and looking like he'd made the worst mistake of his life.

The industrial mixer was whirring at full speed. The giant bag of flour next to it? Wide open. And the blades? Already sending a white cloud of powder straight into the air.

I braced myself for impact, already picturing the headlines: Logan

Richards and Sophie Hartwell: Drenched in Flour at King Cake Disaster Date!

But before the flour could explode over everything, Elizabeth moved. She didn't shout. Didn't flinch. Didn't even look fazed. She stepped forward, smooth as ever, and shut the mixer off with one hand while steadying the bag with the other. She whipped a dish towel off the counter and waved it through the air, sending the cloud drifting away from the workstation instead of straight onto Sophie's perfectly styled dress.

And because Elizabeth thought of everything, she casually nudged Sophie's elbow to turn her away before she even noticed what was happening.

The whole thing lasted five seconds.

By the time Sophie turned back around, smiling, oblivious, tossing her hair like a pro, the mess was gone. Sophie never noticed how close she'd come to disaster. The reporters hadn't caught it either. But I had.

And the young baker? Still standing there, frozen in absolute terror. Elizabeth, clipboard still in hand, turned to him, her voice low and calm. "You okay?"

The kid nodded rapidly, looking like he was one deep breath away from passing out.

She handed him a clean spatula and gave him a quick, reassuring nod. No lecture, no scolding. Just a simple, steady look that said, *Get back to work, you're fine.*

And then, just like that, she was moving again.

Like it was nothing.

Like she hadn't just saved the young baker from an absolute melt-down. Like she hadn't single-handedly prevented a PR disaster in front of a dozen cameras without so much as breaking a sweat.

I wasn't surprised that she was good at her job. I'd seen firsthand how she always had a plan, how she could turn any situation to her advantage. But watching her in action, pulling every thread at the right time, smoothing over every rough edge before anyone even noticed there was one?

That was something else.

I thrived in chaos. I liked the unpredictability of life, the way it cracked and unraveled, the way it kept everyone guessing. Control was suffocating. Control was rules and expectations, and people waiting for you to fail.

But this? This wasn't just control.

This was power.

Elizabeth seemed to move through life with a confidence so effortless it was almost unfair. Every moving piece, every potential problem, she already had a solution before anyone even knew it was needed.

And I hated that I noticed. Hated that it was... kind of hot.

No. Not hot. Just admirable. Yeah. That was it.

But in Elizabeth's interactions with the intern, I caught something else. The way she softened for just a second, her voice losing that sharp efficiency, her expression shifting into something almost gentle. It was quick, barely noticeable, but for the first time, I saw a flicker of something beneath all that control.

And then, just as fast, it was gone.

I didn't know why that stuck with me. But it did.

Once we were finished, I spotted Elizabeth sitting in the hallway, glued to her laptop, probably drafting yet another damage control email.

She was so focused that she didn't even notice me walking up.

I leaned against the doorframe. "You know, for someone who planned this entire thing, you didn't eat anything."

She looked up, startled. "What?"

I held up a paper napkin. Inside, a single, perfectly cut slice of king cake.

Her brows lifted as she peeked under the napkin. "You cut me a piece of cake?"

"I stole it," I corrected. "The bakers were guarding the good pieces, so technically, this is a high-stakes operation."

She snorted. "A criminal and a gentleman."

I grinned. "Don't spread it around. I've got a reputation to protect." Before she could say anything else, I rocked back on my heels. "Anyway, enjoy. You do eat, right? Or do you survive on pure stress?"

She shook her head but took the cake, breaking off a piece and popping it into her mouth.

And maybe it was my imagination, but she looked genuinely touched. She waved me off, chewing, but I caught the tiniest hint of a smile.

And as I turned to go, I glanced back.

Elizabeth was still sitting there, staring down at the napkin like she wasn't sure what had happened.

Truthfully?

Neither was I.

# 11

## ELIZABETH

I WAS SO good at my job that Logan's fake relationship was making headlines in all the right ways. It had only been a week since their first "date" at City Bark, but the press was devouring the narrative we had built. How he and Sophie had been secretly dating for months and were now getting serious. It was almost too easy. And for once, that meant I got a little time off.

Which was why I was finally seeing Jake.

I should've made time for him sooner. I've been back in New Orleans for two weeks, technically staying at his house—our parents' old house—every night, but I left so early and came back so late that I might as well not be there at all. Jake, of course, didn't complain. He never does. But I knew I'd been neglecting him, and it'd been weighing on me.

Jake had been diagnosed with Charcot-Marie-Tooth when we were kids, a genetic nerve disorder that made his muscles weaker over time. He never talked about what it was like to lose muscle, lose stability, lose the ease of movement that most people took for granted. He never asked for help. But I wanted to do what I could to help anyway.

But there was no cure. Not yet.

There were experiments, though. Several using gene therapy have shown early promise. They were hopeful enough that Jake wanted in. But nothing about the process was simple. There were waitlists, approvals, funding, and connections that made the difference between a name on a piece of paper and an actual spot in the program. And that was why I took this job in the first place. Not because I loved PR. Not because I wanted to spend my days managing other people's reputations. But because I needed the kind of connections that could make things like this happen.

But for now, we were waiting to see if he'd been accepted.

And there I was at Sarah's café/bookstore, Inkwell, waiting for my brother to show up.

I flipped through an artist's portfolio that Sarah keeps on a coffee table, sighing as I recognized the work. Max Landreau. I should have bought his paintings before he became popular, but now his prices have skyrocketed, and I can't afford even a postcard.

Sarah slid into the chair across from me, setting down her tea. "Girl, you're staring at that book like it's the last piece of cake at a wedding, and someone else is about to take it."

I sighed dramatically, shutting the portfolio. "Worse. I could've bought his work back when he was selling prints for fifty bucks, but now? A single piece costs more than my rent."

Sarah snickered. "This is why I tell you to buy art when you first see it."

"Yes, let me just hop in a time machine and tell past me to invest in art instead of iced coffee."

Sarah tilted her head, considering. "I mean, you'd still be broke, but at least you'd have something nice to look at."

I narrowed my eyes. "You're supposed to be supportive."

She sipped her tea, unbothered. "I am. But if you keep sulking like that, I might have to ask you to leave because you're bringing down my café's vibe."

I scoffed. "You'd kick me out for bad vibes?"

Sarah shrugged. "I don't make the rules."

I arched a brow. "Uh, yes, you do."

"Fine. I make the rules, so don't worry. You're always the exception."

Before I could say anything, the café door swung open, and Jake walked in. He barely had time to scan the room before Sarah launched out of her chair and threw her arms around him.

"Finally! My favorite customer is here," Sarah said.

Jake chuckled, hugging her back. "If this is the welcome I get, I should show up more often."

Sarah pulled back, grinning. "You already do. At this point, I should give you a frequent flyer card."

I watched them, a little amused and more than a little guilty. Their bond was effortless, built on the kind of daily familiarity I didn't have with Jake anymore. Seeing them like this, so at ease with each other, made my chest ache.

But more than that, it made me grateful. If I couldn't always be here, at least he had Sarah.

Jake turned to me with a teasing glint in his eyes. "So, do I get a hug from you, too, or just the usual thoughtful silence?"

I smiled and leaned over, wrapping my arms around him. He was warm and solid, and for a moment, I wished I could make up for all the time I'd been away.

"Look at this," Sarah said, pressing a hand over her heart. "A historic moment of sibling affection."

I laughed softly, and Jake gave my shoulder a final squeeze before letting go.

Sarah dropped the menus in front of us with an exaggerated sigh. "Well, I'll leave you two to your long-overdue bonding.

After she left, Jake turned to me. "So, tell me, are you staying in the house, or do you need me to set up a forwarding address to your hotel?"

Guilt coiled tight in my chest. I hated that he had to ask. Hated that he wasn't wrong. "I know," I admitted, the words tasting like an apology.

Jake shrugged, easygoing as ever. "C'mon, you know I'm kidding. You're here now. That's what matters."

I wanted to believe that. I did. I watched as he carefully lifted his coffee cup, his hands a little unsteady. I'd seen him struggle before, his hands not quite responding the way he wanted. The slightest tremor in his fingers. The hesitation before he lifted the cup. The way his hand wobbled, just a little, as he brought it to his lips.

The same way Dad's hands had shaken toward the end.

The memory came sharp and sudden, knocking the air from my lungs. Dad struggling to button his shirt, cursing under his breath but smiling anyway, as if he could joke about it, we wouldn't notice how bad it was getting.

The irony, if you could call it that, was that Charcot-Marie-Tooth had nothing to do with his death. Both he and my mother were gone in an instant.

A wreck on I-10.

A storm that came out of nowhere. A driver who never saw my parents' car until it was too late.

Jake and I had been waiting for them to come home, sitting on the couch and watching a ridiculous reality show while texting Mom updates about what we wanted for dinner. She'd sent me a thumbs-up emoji. That was the last thing I ever got from her.

By the time we got the call, it was already too late. There were no goodbyes, no bedside vigil, no time to prepare. Just everything we knew, everything we counted on, ripped out from under us.

And after the shock, after the funeral, after the weeks of people bringing us casseroles we never ate, I had to face the other reality.

Jake had the same disease that Dad had, Charcot-Marie-Tooth.

And now here we were. Years later.

Jake's hands were shaking, just like Dad's had.

There was no cure, but even though it wasn't the same, even though I knew he wasn't dying, it still felt like I was losing him. It felt like I was losing control all over again.

That was why I needed Jake to get into the trial, why I needed to be in control of his future, because if I wasn't... then what?

I needed control.

When our parents died, it was like the floor dropped out from under me. I had no warning, no preparation, no time to brace myself. I spiraled. I stayed in bed for weeks, not because I wanted to, but because I couldn't imagine doing anything else. It was like I'd been unplugged from the world. The fear and the helplessness almost crushed me.

And I swore I would never feel like that again.

A career in PR became the antidote. In PR, I was the one who knew what was coming. I got to manage the message, map the strategy, and prepare for the fallout. I was the person people called when everything was falling apart, and I *made it better*. I couldn't save my parents, I couldn't stop Jake's diagnosis, but I could control everything else. The calendar. The spin. The interviews. The story.

In a world where nothing felt certain, PR gave me a sense of power.

Jake caught me watching him and deliberately set the cup down with exaggerated precision.

His sandy brown hair, a little longer than when I'd last seen him, brushed his shoulders in a way that made him look effortlessly cool rather than unkempt. His brown eyes, sharp and always a little amused, missed nothing. He was brilliant, annoyingly bright, but never in a way that made him seem nerdy. Jake had a way of knowing everything without acting like he needed to prove it.

Jake had always been ridiculously handsome, like our dad. He had the kind of good looks that made people do double-takes.

Just like Logan.

I blinked at the thought, shoving it away before it could take root.

"Okay, stop with the sorrowful look," Jake said. "I'm fine."

I nodded, forcing a smile, but the guilt didn't go away.

Jake filled me in on his physical therapy and how things were going at work. Great, according to him. He was an engineer for the city, a job he loved, and he brushed past the challenges of managing his illness like they were minor inconveniences rather than daily hurdles. That was Jake. If he struggled, he wasn't about to dwell on it.

When he tried to turn the conversation to me, I steered it toward work, shifting the focus to Logan's PR campaign. Work was safe. Work didn't ask uncomfortable questions.

"So, you're turning the bad boy into Prince Charming," Jake teased. "Sounds risky."

I opened my mouth to respond, but hesitated. Would he hear something in my voice? Would he see the way Logan was getting under my skin? I shrugged, aiming for casual. "It's a job."

Jake smirked. "Uh-huh. This PR job seems to involve *a lot* of in-person time."

I took a slow sip of my coffee, choosing my words carefully. "It's a more... hands-on campaign. His public image needs a major reset, and that means making sure the right stories get told, and that people believe them."

He hummed. "Must be pretty bad if it requires *this* much work."

Before I could deflect further, the door jingled.

I didn't even have to turn around because I *felt* it. That shift in the air. The subtle hush, the ripple of attention, the way people instinctively turned toward the door. And when I finally glanced up, there he was.

Logan Fisher strode in like he owned the place, confidence radiating from every step. The black T-shirt, the artful mess of his hair— he had the kind of presence that made people take notice.

And I was noticing.

I clenched my jaw. This was ridiculous. He was my client. I never got distracted by my clients. I'd worked with some of the most powerful men in the world and never once let a pretty face throw me off my game.

And yet.

Jake, watching the scene unfold, turned to me with a look. "Wait. Did you know he was coming?"

I exhaled through my nose. How was I supposed to have a normal conversation with my brother when the most distracting man alive was standing right there?

"Yes. But not yet."

Jake's eyebrows shot up. "So, he came early just to see you?"

I didn't answer my brother, but when Logan reached our table, I said, "You're early."

Logan shrugged, grinning. "I don't think so."

I pulled out my phone to show him the time. "You are."

Logan leaned in slightly, squinting at the screen, and I cursed the way my pulse jumped at his proximity.

Logan turned to Jake, something shifting in his expression. "Wait —is that a Radiators shirt?"

Jake brightened. "Yeah. You know them?"

And they were off, diving into a conversation about music, concerts, and local bands.

Something about the way he and Jake were talking, so effortlessly, so naturally, made my stomach twist. Logan wasn't just charming his way through the conversation. He fit in. He belonged here, in this café, at this table, talking music with my brother.

He was real.

Just like at the dog park. Just like when he brought me that king cake.

And that was a problem. Because I could feel it happening. I was starting to like him.

And I needed to stop. Immediately.

# 12

## LOGAN

I WASN'T mad that I got the time wrong.

Usually, I would be. Normally, I'd be irritated that I'd miscalculated, that I'd wasted time sitting somewhere I didn't need to be. But right then? Sitting across from Elizabeth and her brother, I was enjoying myself. For the first time in a long while, I wasn't counting down the minutes until I could leave.

That was new.

Jake was easy to talk to, sharp but laid-back, the kind of guy who could make a conversation feel like it had already been happening long before you walked in. And this Elizabeth was different from the one I was used to.

I'd only ever known PR Elizabeth, the woman who was all polished and efficient, who carried the weight of everything on her shoulders and refused to let anyone help. The one who looked at me like a mess that she was contractually obligated to clean up.

But here? With Jake? She was something else entirely.

Jake leaned back in his chair, stretching out his legs. "Elizabeth is like a New Orleans summer. She's warm when she wants to be, but don't expect a break from the heat."

Elizabeth scoffed, but her eyes were soft. "And you're like a New

Orleans pothole. Surprisingly deep, constantly underestimated, but always there when you least expect it."

Jake barked out a laugh, shaking his head. "That's the nicest thing you've ever said to me."

Elizabeth smirked. "I'll deny it if you ever bring it up again."

Something tightened in my chest as I watched them.

This was what family looked like. Not just the teasing but the comfort beneath it. The way you could joke with someone because there was no question that, at the end of the day, you'd show up for each other.

Elizabeth was all sharp edges with me, but here? Here, she was something softer, something steadier.

I wasn't sure why I felt the need to stay and watch.

"So, what do you do, man?" I asked, forcing myself to refocus on Jake.

"I'm a civil engineer for New Orleans. Mostly infrastructure projects. It's not as glamorous as a rock star's life, but hey, somebody's gotta keep the roads from swallowing your tour bus whole."

I laughed. "That's fair."

Jake picked up his coffee, but his grip was careful. Too careful.

I wouldn't have thought twice about it except that Elizabeth noticed too. She was watching him, like she wanted to step in but knew better.

Jake took a sip and set the cup down with a little too much control. Then he flexed his fingers, like they didn't quite work the way he wanted them to.

I glanced at Elizabeth again, but she was focused on stirring her coffee, her expression unreadable.

Then, Jake grinned and launched into a story about the time Elizabeth tried to cook an entire Thanksgiving meal by herself in college and nearly set their oven on fire.

"Okay, first of all," Elizabeth cut in, narrowing her eyes, "I was perfectly capable."

Jake snorted. "Liz, the smoke alarm went off three times."

"There were technical difficulties."

"Yeah, like you not knowing how to cook a turkey."

I laughed, watching Elizabeth huff in mock frustration before shaking her head and smiling. The three of us fell into an easy rhythm. Jake telling stories, Elizabeth trying (and failing) to downplay them, and me enjoying the rare sight of her with her guard down.

For once, she wasn't watching me like I was her biggest problem. She was watching me differently. Not with exasperation. Not with barely concealed frustration. But with something softer, something almost... curious. Like she was seeing me in a new light, and maybe not hating what she saw.

And I liked it.

Not just because she was gorgeous—though, yeah, *obviously* that wasn't lost on me. Those sharp, assessing eyes, that effortless confidence that made her impossible to ignore. But it wasn't just that. It was the way she could hold a room without even trying, the way she was so sharp, so quick, so powerful.

And then there were moments like this, when she wasn't working, wasn't strategizing, wasn't two steps ahead of everyone else. When she laughed and let herself be part of the moment instead of controlling it.

I liked that part of her, too. Maybe even more than the rest.

Jake checked his watch and sighed. "Well, gotta get back to work before someone notices I've disappeared." He stood, clapping me on the shoulder with a solid pat, his grip firm despite the effort I now realized it took.

Then he gave me a long look, like he was seeing something he hadn't expected to find.

"You know, Liz," he said, nodding toward her, "I like this guy." He tilted his head at me. "He's not what I expected."

Elizabeth blinked, like she wasn't sure how to respond. Jake chuckled as he grabbed his coffee and headed for the door, walking with a slight limp. I turned to Elizabeth, expecting her to dismiss Jake's comment about me.

But she didn't. Instead, she just looked at me, something unreadable in her expression.

I held her gaze for a beat, then smirked. "Guess I'm full of surprises."

Her faint smile hinted that she might be starting to think the same. But before either of us could acknowledge it, she straightened, all business again.

Ah, there it was. The Great Wall of Elizabeth, back up in record time.

And I hated it.

Because I'd seen the other side of her. The side that was softer, real, right there with me, and I wanted that version of her back.

And instead of that woman, I got sharp edges and clipped efficiency, shutting the door on whatever had just happened between us.

And she'd seen me too. Not as some reckless, image-ruining disaster she had to fix, but as... I don't know. A person. Something beyond a job.

"We need to go over the details for tomorrow night," she said, swiping her screen to life.

I smirked. Fine. If she wanted to act like nothing happened, like we hadn't had a moment, I could play along. "You mean my big romantic evening at Emeril's? Can't wait."

She barely glanced up. "You'll arrive at 7:30 sharp. The car will pull up to the main entrance, where you'll step out first and help Sophie out."

I gave her a slow nod, watching the way she focused, utterly absorbed in her work. That sharp mind, that unwavering control. It was intimidating.

And a little thrilling.

I gave her a slow nod. "Right, right. Big moment. Theatrics. What's my motivation?"

Elizabeth tapped at her screen without looking up. "Pretend you're a functioning adult who understands basic human interactions."

I grinned. There was that famous wit of hers. "That'll be tough."

"You're telling me."

I leaned back in my chair, studying her. The way her fingers moved quickly over the tablet, the way she barely gave me a passing glance. Like I was a job, a task to be managed, and yet, I swore I caught something else—the tiniest flicker of amusement before she smoothed her expression back into neutral.

I asked, "So, what's next? Candlelit dinner?"

"Holding hands across the table. Maybe even"—she scrolled through her notes, then grimaced like she couldn't believe she had to say it—"feeding each other food."

I stared at her. "Oh, that is not happening."

She gave me a tight, expectant smile.

I groaned. "Come on, Elizabeth, even you have to admit that's ridiculous."

"Oh, I absolutely do." Her lips twitched. Man, she almost smiled. Almost. "But the press will eat it up, so unfortunately, so will you."

I folded my arms. "I draw the line at being hand-fed like a zoo animal."

"Well, if you want to get creative, you can suggest something else. But make it look natural, not like you're reading cue cards off a hostage video."

I coughed. "Fine. I'll be the picture of romance." Then I tilted my head. "Wait, you're coaching me through this whole thing, right?"

She blinked. "Obviously."

"So you'll be in my ear the entire night."

She paused. "...Yes."

A slow grin spread across my face. "You sure you want that? Spending your entire evening whispering sweet nothings to me?"

Elizabeth didn't dignify that with a response. She just rolled her eyes and grabbed a scone off the plate between us.

I picked up a bit of my scone and raised an eyebrow. "Hmmm. Maybe I can do the whole feeding and being fed thing. I just need a little practice."

She looked at me thoughtfully, and something in her eyes dared me to keep going.

"Let's see... first, I... lean over? Like this? I tilted forward, closer than necessary, to see what she'd do. "Then I focus on her lips."

Elizabeth didn't move away. If anything, she leaned in, her breath catching. One hand rested on the table, the other brushing the edge of her water glass, like she needed something to hold onto. Her voice was low. "Focus in on her lips, huh?"

Elizabeth's lips were lovely. They were the perfect shade of pink, with a fuller bottom lip that made it unfairly easy to imagine how soft they must be. "And pop this right in?"

As if moving in slow motion, Elizabeth nodded. "J-just like that."

I knew I shouldn't. But I seemed locked into it. So was Elizabeth. She leaned slightly closer across the table, her mouth parting the slightest bit.

No turning back now.

I popped the piece of scone into her mouth. "Like... that?"

Her eyes went wide as she chewed, swallowing slowly. "Y-yes. Like that."

My heart was doing something ridiculous, fluttering like a fool idiot, and the warmth in my chest felt altogether inappropriate for what should have been a casual demonstration.

But then—was she blushing?

Oh yeah. So much.

And that did something to me. We were still staring at each other, neither moving, neither speaking. Then someone cleared their throat.

We both jolted back like we'd been caught committing a crime.

"Yeah, well, I guess I can handle that," I said, forcing a casual shrug.

Elizabeth fumbled for her composure. "Yes. Yeah. I mean, you can. Definitely." Was she flustered? Oh, she was flustered.

I rubbed my chest, trying to ignore the way her pretty pink blush made me feel oddly, stupidly proud.

Then, just as quickly as it had appeared, the moment was gone. Her jaw tightened, and she gave the slightest shake of her head, regaining control. "I am confident that, by the end of the night, you will have successfully convinced the world that you are wildly in love with Sophie Hartwell."

I held her gaze, letting the moment stretch.

Then I smirked. "Guess we'll find out."

She exhaled, stuffing her tablet in her bag. "Just keep the headphones on."

I opened my mouth for another witty remark, but something about the way she said it stopped me. Because here's the thing—I'd planned on ditching the earpiece halfway through for a bit of peace.

But now? Now, I wasn't so sure. Because I liked having Elizabeth in my ear.

# 13

## ELIZABETH

THERE WE WERE at Emeril's restaurant, with cameras flashing outside, reporters elbowing each other for position, and Logan and Sophie seated at the best table in the house.

I sat in a corner, out of the way, pretending to be any other diner, headphones in, listening to every single second of their date. If someone had paid any attention to me, however, they would have thought I was on the phone.

But I wasn't. I was listening to Logan. And that was becoming a problem.

Because I was starting to like Logan Richards.

Not in a *real* way. Not in any way that mattered. Just a little crush. That was all.

It was *annoying* how charming he could be when he wasn't trying to get on my nerves. How effortlessly funny he was—wry, a little self-deprecating, never taking himself too seriously. That was the part I hadn't expected. That, despite his reputation, despite the headlines and the messes I had to clean up, *he had a sense of humor about all of it.*

And, of course, he was gorgeous. That was *objectively* true. He had that sharp, undone kind of handsomeness. Dark brown hair tousled like he'd just run a hand through it for effect. He looked like he'd stepped out of a high-fashion shoot: leather jacket, brooding expression, the kind of guy who bends the whole room to his will without even trying.

But none of that mattered because he was my client.

And crushing on a client? Unprofessional. Unacceptable. I tamped it down before it could turn into something more. This was *nothing*. Just a flicker of misplaced attraction that would be gone before long.

At least, that's what I told myself.

Logan's hand twitched where it rested on the table, but his face stayed perfectly composed. Without missing a beat, he took a sip of his wine and leaned in toward Sophie with that easy, practiced charm.

"You look beautiful," he said.

She giggled. "Thank you for bringing me that lily you picked. You're so romantic."

My breath caught. He had brought her a flower, just as I had told him to do. This was fine. This was precisely what I had planned. So why did it feel like my skin was too tight? Like my pulse was knocking a little too hard against my ribs?

I watched as Logan, so smoothly, leaned closer to Sophie. "So... tell me something real about you. What's a secret most people don't expect when they meet Sophie Hartwell?"

She lit up, laughter spilling out like champagne. There was a softness between them now, the kind of moment that sold a relationship better than any headline ever could.

Logan smiled, settling back. He was present. Charming. Connected. Exactly the version of himself I had been trying to build.

This was good. This was working. If anyone looked over now, they'd be thoroughly convinced. Hook, line, and sinker. I should have been thrilled, but instead I exhaled, forcing my fingers to unclench where they had curled against the table. I was being ridiculous. This was my job.

And yet...

Why did seeing Logan and Sophie giggling make my jaw tighten?

I told myself that it was anxiety. That I just wanted this night to go off without a hitch. That it was professional irritation, nothing more. That I wasn't feeling anything else. Because what else would I be feeling?

Jealousy?

I nearly laughed at the absurdity of it. I wasn't jealous. I was his publicist, for heaven's sake. This wasn't real.

But my stomach clenched anyway.

I forced myself to take a slow sip of my water, schooling my face into a picture of neutral calm, reminding myself that any real professional wouldn't be sitting here, gripping their glass so tightly that it might shatter.

Then Logan turned back to Sophie, nodding at his plate.

"And hey, this broccolini is fantastic. Would you like a bite?"

Sophie smiled and nodded: "I'd love that."

He plucked a spear and offered it to her. My chest tightened. Not with jealousy, I told myself, but pride. He was doing exactly what I recommended.

Then Sophie reached for her plate. "Would you like some of my escargot?"

Logan didn't hesitate. "Yes, please." He closed his eyes like she was bestowing a gift from the heavens.

She grinned and dropped one right into his mouth.

The sight of it made my stomach flip.

And before I could stop myself, I said, "You're a lucky man. Most people have to wait until they're in assisted living to get spoon-fed in public."

Silence.

Oh no. What was I *doing*?

I was supposed to be the calm, professional voice in his ear, not... whatever *that* was. Jealousy? Panic? Possession? Whatever it was, it was mortifying. I needed to shut up before I derailed the whole night.

But Logan didn't look annoyed. Quite the opposite. His jaw twitched, eyes gleaming with barely suppressed laughter as he chewed with exaggerated pleasure, clearly enjoying every second of my meltdown.

"You know," he said to Sophie, swirling his wine, "I never told you the kind of woman I'm into."

This was my moment to recover. I adjusted my earpiece and leaned forward slightly, whispering the exact script into his earpiece like a seasoned producer feeding a teleprompter. "Honey-blonde hair. Dimples. Blue eyes. All-American girl-next-door."

He leaned back. "It's not about looks," he said smoothly.

I frowned. That was *not* in the script. "Wait, what?" The words slipped out before I could stop them.

Logan carried on like he hadn't heard me. "I like a woman who can keep up, you know? Someone smart, sharp. A little unpredictable."

Sophie smiled, twirling the stem of her wine glass between her fingers. "Mysterious?"

Logan tilted his head. "Not mysterious, exactly." He paused, then sighed like he was suddenly waxing poetic. "I think the best kind of girl... is like a New Orleans summer."

My stomach flipped. I nearly choked on my water. No. Absolutely not. Was he recycling lines from my brother? I stared at him, pulse kicking up. What in the world was he doing?

Sophie blinked, intrigued. "A New Orleans summer?"

Logan exhaled, his expression thoughtful. "Warm when she wants to be"—he casually lifted his glass—"and there's no break from the heat."

I went still. Heat curled in my chest.

Sophie laughed, delighted. "I love that."

But Logan wasn't looking at her.

For half a second, his gaze flicked to me. It was so quick that I almost convinced myself I had imagined it.

Something in my grip tightened.

Oh. Oh no.

I had gotten used to Logan flirting in a controlled environment, when I was safely out of the line of fire. But this? This was something else entirely. Because when he looked at me like that, when he borrowed words that had once been used to describe me, it made my skin feel too warm. It made my pulse jump in a way I refused to acknowledge.

I forced myself to breathe, gripping the table as if it were the only thing anchoring me to reality. Sophie was still smiling, sipping her wine, utterly unaware of the chaos happening in my head. I swallowed hard and pressed two fingers to my earpiece.

"Logan," I said in his ear, my voice deceptively calm. "I will kill you."

"Warm like a New Orleans summer." He smiled at Sophie as if she were the most fascinating person in the room. "Have you ever met someone like that?"

"Logan," I hissed again.

When Logan turned back to Sophie, amusement still glinting in his eyes, something about it felt different.

He wasn't looking at her like she was the one sharing the joke. He was looking at me, like he wanted me to react as if he were waiting for my response.

Oh, drat. I swallowed, shifting in my seat. This was fine. I was fine.

Sophie giggled, nudging the fork toward his mouth again. "I think I do know someone like that."

Across the restaurant, Logan kept glancing toward me.

Not subtly, either, like some rookie at a poker table who'd never learned to keep his tells in check.

And he was doing it often enough that Sophie noticed. She followed his gaze, her brow furrowing slightly before she covered it with another bright, camera-ready smile. "You're lucky your PR person isn't as scary as mine is."

I stiffened. Nope. This wasn't good. She wasn't wrong. I was his PR person, and I was supposed to be detached. Except now I was sitting there, in a very expensive restaurant, suddenly feeling very attached.

Sophie excused herself to the bathroom, flashing Logan a playful smile as she slid out of her seat.

I took the opportunity to exhale, to reset, to remind myself that this was work. That whatever tension was crackling between Logan and me wasn't real, just collateral damage from spending too much time in each other's heads.

But before I could even remind Logan to stay in character, he leaned forward, voice low. "You okay over there?"

"I'm just fine," I muttered. "Stop talking to me."

"Why?" he murmured, still pretending to focus on his wine. "I like our little chats."

"Because though I look like I'm on the phone, you look like a fool talking to yourself."

He stilled, then he began timing his words with natural movements. He took a slow sip of wine, exhaling as if considering something important, and shook his head slightly. "You sure you're okay? Because you sound a little flustered."

"I'm not flustered."

"Mm. Could've fooled me."

"Logan—"

He stretched out his legs under the table, completely at ease. "Just saying," he murmured, "you seemed to really like that line about a woman being like a New Orleans summer."

"I liked it when *Jake* said it. You butchered it beyond recognition."

He grinned, swirling his drink. "I think you do like it."

I groaned. *This man.*

He kept his voice low enough that only I could hear. "You know, you should relax and enjoy yourself. You're getting very invested in my date."

I clenched my jaw. "I'm invested in making sure you don't mess this up," I shot back.

"Mmm." He smirked, hiding his mouth as he adjusted his cufflink. "If you say so."

I was about to respond—probably with something that would get me fired—when I realized something.

Sophie had been gone a long time. Too long.

I frowned. "I'm going to check on Sophie."

Logan hummed. "Jealous?"

"Over you? Never. But if she ditched you in the middle of your date, I'd like to know before TMZ does." I stood and made my way to the bathroom, already preparing myself for whatever nonsense I was about to walk into. The second I stepped inside, I heard her.

Sophie's voice was low but clear. "Babe, I know."

I froze. Then, I took one step closer.

"No, it's not like that," she murmured. "You're overthinking this." A pause. A sigh, frustrated but familiar, like this wasn't the first time she'd had this conversation. "I told you, it's fine." Another beat. "I just, ugh, can we talk later?" Silence. Then, softer. "Come on, babe, don't be like that."

I pressed my lips together. Okay. That could mean anything.

But given the fact that she was supposed to be Logan's devoted, adoring girlfriend—and she was currently in a bathroom whispering "babe" to someone who wasn't him—it didn't sound great. It would have been disastrous if somebody else had heard her.

The call ended, and before I could pretend I wasn't standing outside her bathroom stall like a detective in a bad crime drama, Sophie swung the door open.

We locked eyes.

I folded my arms. "I heard you talking. To 'babe.'" My voice was calm and measured. "You need to stay committed to this relationship."

Sophie didn't even blink. Instead, she smirked, looking in the mirror to freshen her lipstick. "It's just a friend."

I arched an eyebrow.

She let out a dramatic sigh, finally turning to face me. "I call everyone 'babe,' babe."

I studied her, trying to decide if she was lying or if she genuinely didn't care that she was risking this entire operation.

She breezed past me, but then—right before she walked back into the restaurant—she turned and tilted her head, studying me like I was a puzzle she suddenly wanted to solve. "Okay, fine. I'll keep playing my part. But tell me something, Elizabeth."

I stiffened. "What?"

Her eyes sparkled, too darn perceptive. "What exactly is going on with you and Logan?"

I scoffed. "Nothing."

Sophie hummed, clearly not buying it. "Sure doesn't seem like *nothing.*"

I forced a dry smile. "Well, it is."

She shrugged, looking entirely unconvinced.

I sat back down at my table, watching as Sophie returned to Logan. He shot me one glance before refocusing on her.

I sipped my wine, ignoring the heat in my chest.

## 14

## LOGAN

No visit to Louisiana is complete without a swamp tour.

So, that's what Sophie and I were doing for our next fake date.

I adjusted my sunglasses, stepping onto the boat as the humid air wrapped around me like a damp blanket.

The boat was a flat-bottomed pontoon, wide and low, with faded green paint and a canopy that appeared to have been patched a few times too many. It was big enough for probably a dozen people, including our entourage and the press. The boat was tied to a crooked wooden dock that wobbled underfoot, sun-bleached and damp in spots. A cooler rattled near the helm, and someone had duct-taped a plastic chair to the bow like it was an upgrade. Not exactly luxury, but it would float.

Behind me, Mick was annoyingly unbothered by the heat. The man looked like he belonged at a rooftop cocktail bar, not trudging through a marsh. His linen shirt was rolled up just so, his designer sunglasses perched perfectly, and somehow, not a single drop of sweat dared touch him.

"This is a terrible idea," I muttered under my breath.

Mick snorted. "Oh yeah, real rough. Having to spend a day on the water, soaking up the culture."

I shot him a look. "If by culture, you mean getting eaten alive by mosquitoes while dodging prehistoric murder lizards, then sure, sounds great."

He patted my shoulder. "That's the spirit, rock star."

To be fair, I wasn't entirely dreading it. Maybe I was just looking forward to seeing Elizabeth.

And there she was.

I was leaning against the side rail when I saw her. Elizabeth stepped onto the dock like she owned it, eyes sharp and taking everything in. Even here—surrounded by swampland, buzzing mosquitoes, and the faint smell of something dead in the water—she looked composed. Capable. Like nothing could throw her off.

Her hair was pulled back into a twist, but the heat had already started working on it. Tiny curls clung to her temples, soft and out of place in a way that felt unfairly distracting.

That shouldn't have been something I noticed. And yet, there I was. Noticing. I exhaled, adjusting my grip on the railing, trying to ignore the way my pulse kicked up a notch when she turned her head and caught me watching.

She didn't say anything. Just arched a single, perfect eyebrow.

I looked away quickly, just in time to see Sophie teeter down the dock. To say she wasn't dressed for a swamp tour was an understatement. Pink platform sandals, a white sundress that probably cost more than the boat itself, and—was that a hat with a *veil*? Like she was heading to a royal garden party instead of a ride through gator-infested marsh.

She wobbled slightly as she stepped onto the deck, gripping my arm with a hiss. "You didn't tell me this would be so... so gross."

Elizabeth's voice cut in smoothly. "It's not a red-carpet event, but that's part of the charm."

I turned back in time to see her smiling. Not her professional, I-have-everything-under-control smile. A real one.

Something in my chest tightened.

Sophie shot her an exasperated look. "I don't know! I thought it would be... less muddy?" She smoothed the front of her dress, as if that would help. "Why didn't you warn me?"

Then, low enough for only me to hear, Mick muttered, "I assumed common sense would do the heavy lifting."

I smothered a laugh as Sophie turned away. But my attention was still stuck on Elizabeth.

Out of the corner of my eye, I saw several photographers step onto the boat. Then our guide clomped onto the boat with the confidence of a man who had seen some things.

"Name's Cajun Cal." He tipped his hat, a well-worn thing adorned with mock alligator teeth. His skin was sun-kissed to a deep brown, his eyes sharp with amusement as he scanned our group—me, Elizabeth, Sophie, Mick, and a handful of photographers—like he was sizing us up. "By the time we're done, you'll know all about gators and what not to do if you fall overboard."

"Wait," Sophie cut in. "People fall overboard?"

Cal just winked.

Sophie muttered something under her breath and tightened her grip on my arm.

We hadn't even left the dock when Cal pointed to the shore. "Looky there, got ourselves a big ol' gator already."

Sure enough, a massive alligator lay half-submerged near the bank, eyes barely above the waterline.

Sophie shuddered. "This is so not necessary."

Then, as if this tour wasn't already on thin ice, Cal reached into a small cooler and pulled out a baby alligator.

"For those of y'all brave enough, we got a little fella here for a photo-op."

Sophie wrinkled her nose. "I'll pass."

Before I could make a joke, Elizabeth spoke to me. "You should hold it."

I scoffed. "You want to see me get bitten."

"No, I want to see if you scream like a child when it moves."

"Challenge accepted." I sighed, trying for nonchalance, but I couldn't suppress the edge of a smile. It was ridiculous, but something about the sting of her teasing got under my skin. I reached out and took the baby gator. It was surprisingly light, its belly cool and smooth against my palm.

Sophie watched warily, then sighed. "Fine. Give it to me."

I handed it over, and for about three seconds, everything was fine.

Then the gator twitched, Sophie screamed, and the baby alligator launched itself onto the deck.

Chaos. Pure. Utter. Chaos.

The photographers scattered first, practically vaulting onto the dock. Mick scrambled after them. Sophie shrieked and jumped into Mick's arms, who immediately buckled under her weight and stumbled back.

Meanwhile, Cal was *not* amused. "Get Lil' Gumbo!" he bellowed, lunging for the loose gator.

I should have moved. Should have done *something*. But I didn't.

Because Elizabeth was already on it. While everyone else panicked, she stayed on the boat, crouched low, and in one smooth motion, scooped up the gator like it was *nothing*. One hand securing its belly, the other casually pressing over its snout.

No hesitation. No flinching. No fear.

My heart slammed against my ribs.

She barely seemed winded as she adjusted her grip, arching an eyebrow at the mess unfolding around her. "You've got to hold 'em right," she said, voice calm despite the absolute *bedlam* on the dock. "Otherwise, they get ideas."

Cal stomped forward, shaking his head as he took the baby gator from her. "Fool city people," he muttered.

Sophie, still clinging to Mick, let out a dramatic breath. "You know what? No. I am done with this. I'm not going."

Cal barely spared her a glance. "Fine by me."

Elizabeth frowned. "Cal, she *has* to come. That was the agreement."

Cal huffed. "Nope. She's not coming."

Elizabeth's eyes narrowed. "The whole point of this is for the press to get photos of *both* of them enjoying the swamp together."

Cal shrugged. "Nah. Gator nearly got loose 'cause of her, and I don't take liabilities on my boat."

Elizabeth inhaled sharply, clearly scrambling to find another angle. "Okay, but look at it this way. She's fine now, she's calmer—"

Sophie cut her off, shaking her head. "No. I am *not* calm, and I am *not* going."

Elizabeth's mouth pressed into a thin line. She turned back to Cal. "Listen, I can promise you she won't cause any more issues."

Cal already had one hand on the throttle. "Not riskin' it."

The boat engine roared to life, and then we were off, leaving Sophie, the photographers, and the baby gator disaster behind.

I turned to Elizabeth, and she turned to me. For a second, neither of us said anything. We just looked at each other like we'd both realized at the same moment that we were now alone, on a boat, in the middle of the swamp.

Well. This just got interesting.

We were both still standing at the back of the boat, and I glanced at the dock. Sophie looked much more at ease on solid ground, already talking with dramatic hand gestures. I caught my name drifting across the water, followed by her giving an exaggerated shake of her head like she was deeply, tragically concerned for my well-being. Elizabeth raised an eyebrow. I didn't comment.

Sophie gasped, throwing a hand over her mouth like she was watching us get dragged away to our doom. "Oh no," she said, voice a touch too rehearsed. "I *hope* Logan will be okay out there. What if something happens?"

Elizabeth cleared her throat and called to Cal. "So, what, you're taking us on a tour anyway?"

Cal shrugged. "Got the boat. Got the swamp. Might as well." Then he gave me a squinty, disapproving once-over. "Besides, the boy looks like he could stand to learn a thing or two."

Elizabeth faced the water, and we both leaned against the railing.

"At least Sophie's playing the supportive, caring girlfriend. That'll get us some points."

I whispered, "Why did you let Cajun Cal take us out here? Usually, you strong-arm people into doing what you want."

"Usually," she murmured, glancing at Cal, who was grumbling to himself. "But I also know when to pick my battles. "Because Cajun Cal runs on his own time, and if I try to tell him otherwise, he'll probably drop us off in the middle of the swamp and let nature take its course."

The boat rocked as Cal maneuvered us through the narrow waterways, Spanish moss dripping from the trees, the heavy scent of earth and water thick in the air.

The boat tilted slightly as we hit a wake, and Elizabeth grabbed my arm. It was instinct, the kind of quick reaction she probably didn't even register. But I sure as heck did.

She laughed, squeezing my arm before letting go. "Careful, rock star, wouldn't want to end up as gator bait."

I swallowed, still feeling the heat of her fingers.

We drifted deeper into the swamp, the hum of insects surrounding us, the occasional ripple in the water betraying something moving beneath the surface.

Cal muttered something about feeding the gators and tossed a piece of meat over the side. A second later, a gator's head broke the water, snatching it up with a sharp snap of its jaws.

Elizabeth leaned forward, eyes bright. "That's incredible."

Suddenly, I wasn't watching the swamp anymore. I was watching her. The way she lit up, wholly absorbed in the moment, her usual composure slipping just enough for me to see something real beneath it.

"It is incredible," I said, and I wasn't talking about the swamp.

She turned toward me, still smiling. "See? Not so bad."

I cleared my throat, forcing my gaze away. "So... gator-wrangling? How'd you become an expert in that?"

Elizabeth's fingers tapped the boat's railing as she gazed out at the swamp. I lingered beside her, sensing something was about to shift, but I didn't know what.

Finally, she turned, her eyes softer, her voice gentler. "My dad used to bring my brother and me out here," she said, her voice touched by nostalgia. "He'd tell us stories—about how wild and unpredictable the swamp is, but how beautiful... if you learned to respect it."

She paused, and I waited. Then the name slipped out quietly. "Jake... you met him, my brother. He has Charcot-Marie-Tooth syndrome. It's a nerve disorder. There's no cure, but I try to help when I can." She let out a breath, her fingers tracing the edge of the railing. "Not that he ever asks for it."

She glanced at me, then away, like she wasn't sure why she was saying any of this.

"You probably noticed something was off with him," she added after a beat, her voice quieter now. "Most people do, even if they don't know what they're seeing. The way he holds things, how he moves. It's subtle, but it's there."

I watched her carefully, noting the subtle shift in her posture. She hadn't planned on saying that. "Sounds like he's lucky to have you."

She let out a small huff, but there wasn't any bite to it. "He'd argue otherwise."

I looked out at the endless stretch of water, the tangled roots rising from below, the way the swamp seemed both vast and closed in at the same time. I knew what it felt like to want to help someone who didn't always want your help. "Yeah," I said finally. "I get that."

She turned to me like she hadn't expected me to agree. Like she hadn't expected me to see what she saw.

I glanced back at her, then away again, feeling something shift in my chest. "I saw you with him at the café." The words came out before I could stop them. "The way you were with him. How close you are. I wanted that."

Her brows furrowed slightly. "Wanted what?"

I hesitated, then shrugged. What was the point in dodging it? "A family. Or maybe just someone who feels like family."

She opened her mouth like she was about to respond, something unreadable flickering across her face. But before she could say anything, the boat lurched beneath us.

It wasn't dramatic, just a sudden, sharp shift that sent her stumbling forward. But we were near the edge, and the water wasn't exactly forgiving.

And then, because the universe had a real sense of humor, a gator surfaced right next to the boat, its dark eyes barely breaking the waterline. A low, rumbling growl filled the air, deep enough that I felt it in my chest.

Panic shot through me. My hand shot out, grabbing her waist and yanking her back before my brain could even catch up.

She gasped, colliding against me, her hands bracing against my chest, her breath warm against my neck. Her eyes were wide with surprise.

Then, of course, she laughed. "Relax, city boy," she teased, breathless but already regaining her balance. "I wasn't going to fall in."

I should have stepped back, cracked a joke, and brushed it off. But I didn't.

And I didn't let go of her immediately. Because here's the thing—my heart was still racing. And not from the gator.

From how right it felt to hold her. Her waist beneath my hands, the way she had gripped me instinctively.

Neither of us spoke.

Then Cal, completely unfazed, called out from the back of the boat, "Well, if y'all wanted a honeymoon package, ya shoulda said somethin'."

Elizabeth let out a sharp breath. "Oh, so hilarious," she deadpanned, angling herself away from me abruptly.

The moment passed, but something in my chest hadn't caught up yet.

As the tour wound down and the boat slowly turned back toward the dock, I found myself watching Elizabeth, noticing the way the wind tugged at the loose strands of her hair, sunlight catching in them, turning them to gold.

I'd spent a lot of time with Elizabeth. Late-night meetings, strategy calls where she was always the sharpest person in the room. And I'd started seeing a different version of her: with her brother at the café, showing me her softer side, that she was more than just a workaholic PR genius.

But on the boat, I saw even more. She had been more relaxed, for once. More unguarded.

And more undeniably... kissable.

# 15

## ELIZABETH

APPARENTLY, after the swamp tour debacle, Sophie had decided her next date needed to happen on solid ground.

Enter: a curated stroll through the Bywater Art District, designed to showcase the happy couple's *cultured* side.

And it was a good idea.

For one reason: Because there was no way, on this well-lit, crowded art walk, that Logan and I would get caught alone together like we had on the swamp tour.

Which was for the best. It was becoming increasingly difficult to deny the *little* crush I had on him.

I trailed a few steps behind them, watching Logan—the world's most reluctant modern art enthusiast—attempt to appreciate modern expressionism.

"Oh wow," he deadpanned, staring at an abstract canvas streaked with jagged slashes of red. "This one speaks to me."

Sophie lit up. "Right? It's so bold! So emotional!"

Logan sighed like he was shouldering a great burden. "But, you know, it's also... moving. Makes you think."

Sophie gasped. "I *knew* you were an art lover, Lo!"

I snorted.

And yet, Sophie was all in. Bless her theatrical little heart.

She pulled Logan to pose in front of every mural, turning the afternoon into a full-fledged photoshoot. A massive, neon-pink alligator? Sophie clung to Logan's arm like they were starring in an indie rom-com. A wall of oversized pop-art lips? She made Logan blow her a kiss for the camera, then demanded a retake because he "wasn't selling it."

To his credit, Logan played along. Kind of.

I stood off to the side, quietly enjoying the spectacle.

Then Sophie's phone chimed. She gasped, clutching Logan's arm like she'd just received a royal decree. "Oh no! I have to take this. It's about the Paris Film Festival. Huge opportunity."

Logan perked up instantly. "You should take it."

Sophie flashed the cameras one last dazzling smile, then skittered off to find a quieter spot, leaving Logan standing beside a trombone made of old car parts, looking mildly relieved.

And then he was walking toward me. His gaze locked on me, eyes narrowing in that way that felt like he was mapping me out, half-smile tugging at one corner of his mouth. It was a deliberate flirtation that made my pulse thud in my throat.

I stiffened. No. Not here. This was Sophie's date, not mine.

"You need to talk to Sophie," I said before he could even open his mouth. "She's your date."

Logan let out a low sigh, rubbing a hand down his face. "Elizabeth—"

"No." I held up a finger, trying to reclaim the ground he'd stolen. "Go back to her."

"I'd rather talk to you."

My stomach dipped. I hated that reaction. Hated that his low, gravelly voice sent heat curling low in my stomach.

I crossed my arms. "Logan, be careful. There are photographers everywhere. You need to act like this is a magical, romantic date."

He tilted his head slightly, gaze flickering over my face. "And how do I do that, oh wise PR guru?"

I sighed, stepping closer and lowering my voice so only he could hear, but trying to make it look as professional as possible.

"You should talk loudly enough that the press can hear," I directed. "Tell her that dating her has been the most fun you've had in a long time. Say you admire how spontaneous she is, how you never know what she's going to do next, but that's what makes being with her exciting. Then, if you want extra credit, tell her she makes you feel happy."

Logan's mouth ticked up at the corner, his eyes flashing with something unreadable. "Man, Elizabeth. Have you ever considered using your powers for evil?"

I rolled my eyes, noticing that Sophie was off the phone. "Go."

He sighed, but he went.

And I watched, arms crossed, as Logan did exactly what I told him to do.

And worse? It worked.

Sophie melted, laughing as Logan twirled her under his arm, all smiles and glittering eyes, as she clung to his jacket as if he were the most fascinating person in the world. The cameras loved it.

I should have been thrilled. This was precisely what I'd wanted. I wanted everyone to think that Logan and Sophie were truly in love. So, even though I knew it was fake, as I watched them looking all lovey-dovey, I should have been happy.

Instead, a stupid, nagging thought wedged itself in my brain: I was making him too good of a fake boyfriend.

I pushed that out of my head fast and focused on trailing behind, making sure everything stayed on track.

Sophie kept enthusiastically leading Logan toward various art installations, and I let myself drift, checking that the press was getting all the right shots.

And then, almost without realizing it, I stopped in front of a painting. It was a landscape of the swamp, done in broad, textured strokes. In the picture, deep blues, hazy greens, and golden light spilled through moss-draped trees. The artwork felt alive, as if you stepped too close, you might hear the hum of cicadas or catch the scent of damp earth.

For some reason, I couldn't look away.

"See something you like?"

My breath caught. It was Logan, and he was too close. Again.

I turned, finding him beside me, hands in his pockets, a casual stance that didn't match the way he was watching me.

"It's fine," he said before I could say anything. "She's on the phone."

I blinked. "What?"

"Sophie." He nodded toward where she stood a few feet away, gesturing dramatically as she talked. "She's busy. So, you know..." His smirk was lazy, effortless. "I'm allowed to talk to my publicist. I'm allowed to talk to you."

Something about the way he said it sent a jolt through my chest, like I'd been caught doing something I wasn't supposed to. Which was ridiculous. I wasn't doing anything. I shook my head as if I were shaking away cobwebs. "I'm appreciating the art."

"I didn't know you were the type."

"What do you mean?"

"The type to slow down long enough to appreciate something just because it's beautiful."

The words hit somewhere they shouldn't.

Logan tilted his head, finally flicking his eyes back to the canvas. "That looks like where we were in the swamp."

"Yeah, it reminds me of my dad." My voice caught, but I powered through. "The artist is Max Landreau. Isn't it gorgeous? I wish I could afford it. Maybe someday."

Logan was quiet for a beat, long enough that I could feel the weight of whatever thought he was turning over in his head. "You liked it out there on the swamp tour, didn't you?" His voice was softer now, like he already knew the answer.

I swallowed. "Yeah. I did."

For a second, I almost said more. Nearly told him how the swamp felt like home in a way I couldn't explain, how the smell of cypress and the hum of tree frogs reminded me of being a kid, trailing behind my dad as he pointed out the way the water shifted with the wind.

But I didn't.

Instead, I shrugged, keeping it light. "Even with the whole 'gator incident.'"

Logan huffed out a laugh. "See? That's why I don't trust nature. Too many teeth."

I smirked, but something about his expression made my stomach twist. He was still watching me, not in a flirtatious way, but like he was *seeing* something I didn't mean to show.

I turned back to the painting, pretending to study the brushstrokes, hoping he'd let it go.

He didn't. "You know," he said, voice low, "just because you can't afford it doesn't mean you can't have it."

I snorted. "What, are you going to steal it for me?"

Logan smirked. "Nah, I prefer not to be arrested on first dates."

I shifted my weight, but my heart did something stupid in my chest. *First date.* He was joking, obviously. But still.

I opened my mouth to change the subject, to pull us out of whatever this was, but Sophie's voice sliced through the moment.

"Lo! Come on, let's take a picture in front of this one!"

Logan held my gaze for a second longer, then he turned and went back to her.

I exhaled slowly, forcing myself to focus as I watched them pose for the cameras.

Sophie laughed, looping her arms around his neck, smiling so effortlessly, like this was all real.

And I felt something I wasn't supposed to feel.

Longing.

# 16

## LOGAN

MUSIC HAD ALWAYS BEEN the one thing that made sense to me.

I exhaled slowly, my fingers drifting over the piano keys, playing through the chords again and adjusting the weight of each note until they felt right. The studio was warm and dimly lit, the air carrying the faint scent of coffee and cologne.

For a while, Mick had been there, cracking jokes and pretending he wasn't hovering to make sure I rehearsed. Elizabeth had arrived a little after him, still in her blazer, tablet in hand, multitasking like her life depended on it. I think she thought Mick would stick around. Heck, I'd assumed the same. But then he'd gotten a call, muttered something about a "vendor emergency," and ducked out with a promise to be back soon.

That had been over thirty minutes ago.

Now, it was just us. The only sounds were the quiet hum of the city beyond the windows, the soft tapping of Elizabeth's fingers against her tablet, and the occasional rustle of fabric as she moved.

She was getting ready for a charity gala while I rehearsed. I'd agreed to perform at a benefit for the local animal shelter—a small, intimate event with a live auction and a cocktail hour, where I'd play a stripped-down set to help raise money. It was something that mattered, and Elizabeth had thrown herself into making sure it was perfect.

The studio felt different with just the two of us. Comfortable. Easy.

She was perched on the edge of the couch, scrolling through her tablet, all business, while I ran through the chords again. The whole setup felt nice. The quiet hum of the city outside, the warmth of the dim lighting, the casual rhythm of her flipping through pages while I played.

Familiar, even. Like we'd done this a hundred times before.

Which was dangerous.

Because the more I got used to this—*to her*—the harder it was getting to pretend I didn't want more.

So, there she was, double-checking details, flipping between event schedules and whatever other plans she had running through her head.

And I was trying not to get distracted by how beautiful she was. And how close she was.

Elizabeth barely looked up from her tablet. "I need you to be on your best behavior tomorrow."

I grinned, leaning back against the piano bench. "Define 'best.'"

She still didn't look at me. "Not getting banned from the venue for throwing a statue would be a good start."

I pressed a hand to my chest. "That was *one* time. And, in my defense, how was I supposed to know that statue wasn't bolted down?"

Now she did look up, brow raised. "Because it was made of ice."

I shrugged. "Hindsight is twenty-twenty."

Elizabeth glanced up at me, and for a second, something softened in her expression—something like amusement, like she was fighting back a smile. Her expression sent something warm through me. I loved making her smile, loved these moments when she let herself enjoy me, just a little.

Then, just as quickly, she schooled her face back into something unimpressed and returned to her screen. "Unbelievable."

It shouldn't have made me grin like an idiot. But it did. "In my defense, it was a *deeply* boring event. Most people would've left early if I hadn't livened things up."

Elizabeth pinched the bridge of her nose like she was reconsidering her entire life. "You and Sophie will pose for the cameras. You'll dance. You'll be introduced after the auction. You'll play three songs, smile for the cameras. That's it. *Easy-peasy.*"

I nodded solemnly. "Right. So what I'm hearing is: *improvise.*"

Her eye twitched. "This is a very different audience than you're used to."

"Yeah," I said, stretching my arms over my head. "No one's throwing beer at me. No one's lighting up in the front row. Feels unnatural."

She shot me a warning look. "Let's keep it that way."

I leaned in conspiratorially. "I don't know. Rich people get *feisty* when they lose a silent auction. I'm just saying, if some hedge fund guy gets outbid on a golden retriever puppy, we *could* have drama."

Her lips twitched like she was holding back a laugh. She shook her head and went back to her tablet, flipping through her notes, all professional again. "Just... read the room, okay?"

I grinned. "I *always* read the room. It's not my fault the room usually wants a show."

I watched her for a second, taking in the way she tucked her hair behind her ear, the way she bit her lip when she was concentrating.

She was gorgeous.

And funny. And smart. And so close.

I dragged my fingers over the piano keys, trying to play it cool, but my pulse was racing.

Hanging out with her, teasing her, watching her *almost* smile was too easy. Too fun. Too... *something.*

I turned back to the piano and played the same section of the song again, letting the melody fill the space between us.

She said quietly, "You've played that same section five times."

"Yeah?" I smirked. "And?"

She hesitated. "It's good."

"That sounded dangerously close to a compliment."

A flicker of a smile.

I should have left it at that. But instead, I said, "Come here."

Elizabeth blinked. "What?"

I nodded toward the piano bench. "Sit."

She let out a soft, disbelieving laugh. "I don't play the piano."

"I didn't ask if you played." I scooted over, making room for her. "Come on. You micromanage everything else in my life, so you might as well see if you can improve my playing, too."

She hesitated. I could see the wheels turning in her head. She was calculating the risk, weighing the pros and cons.

Then, finally, she moved. The second she sat beside me, warmth radiated between us. My pulse skipped.

She smelled like coffee and lavender.

Not distracting. Not at all.

"Okay," I said, tilting my head. "I know you're a control freak, so just press a key. Any one."

Elizabeth shot me a look. "I'm not a control freak."

I snorted. "Elizabeth, you color-code your emails."

She sighed, but then lifted a hand and pressed a key. A single, simple note.

Her fingers brushed mine, and it was like a live wire shot through me.

I didn't pull away.

The air shifted. Her breath caught slightly, and I heard it, felt it. She was close enough that if I just turned—

No. I couldn't. Shouldn't.

But she wasn't moving away either.

The air between us felt charged. The faint scent of coffee and lavender curled around me, and she was so close, just a breath away. If I leaned in—

BEEP! BEEP! BEEP!

Elizabeth jolted like she'd been shocked, fumbling for her phone as the alarm blared between us.

"Seriously?" I exhaled, half-murderous toward whatever had just ruined the moment.

Elizabeth's eyes widened as she silenced the alarm. "Oh. Right. I, uh, I set a reminder."

I arched a brow, fighting back a smirk. "For what?"

She shot me a glare, cheeks slightly pink. "To check the final auction item list before the event."

I let out a short laugh, running a hand through my hair. "You schedule everything, huh?"

"It's my job," she muttered, but there was something softer about her voice now, something almost flustered.

I watched her for a moment, the weight of what almost happened still hanging in the air. She had felt it too. I knew she had.

But then, she was all business again, tapping furiously at her screen as if she hadn't just been centimeters away from kissing me.

I exhaled, fingers drifting back over the piano keys, letting the melody fill the space between us.

Elizabeth cleared her throat. "You know, I don't get you."

"Yeah? Join the club."

But she didn't laugh. Instead, she rested her hands on her lap, watching me. "Why did you sabotage your career? Why are you like this?"

I arched a brow. "Like what?"

She exhaled. "Rebellious. Reckless." Her voice softened, like she wasn't just saying it to scold me. "Like you want to be self-destructive."

I didn't answer right away. Not because I didn't know. But because, for the first time in a long time, I wanted to answer. I hit a few soft chords, my voice quieter. "I spent my whole life being told who I was supposed to be."

Elizabeth didn't interrupt.

"I was the son of a legend, which meant I had to be a certain way, sound a certain way, act a certain way. When I finally got my career, I didn't know how to separate myself from all that. And then... when my dad got sick..."

I stopped. Jaw tightening.

Oh no.

I shouldn't have said that.

Even to her. Something told me that I could trust her, but it wasn't public information, and I wasn't ready to talk about it.

Elizabeth's posture shifted. Subtle, but I felt it. Her focus sharpened, like she was mentally rewinding my words, picking them apart.

"Sick?" She was watching me too closely now, and I didn't like that. Didn't like the way her expression softened, like she saw through me for a second.

I needed to shut this down. I cleared my throat, shifting on the bench. "What about you?" I kept my tone light. Casual. Deflecting. "Why are you like this?"

Her brows furrowed. "Like what?"

"Workaholic. Uptight. Afraid to take a breath without scheduling it first."

She scoffed, but there was less bite to it than usual. "Someone has to keep things together. I can't afford to lose control."

I tilted my head. "Why?"

She hesitated. And for the first time, she didn't have an answer.

The silence stretched, warm and charged.

And then, as if she suddenly realized how close we were, how easily this moment could turn into something else, like it almost had before, she shifted back.

Her voice was crisp again. "Anyway, this was fun, but the charity event is tomorrow, and I still have work to do."

She gathered her things, preparing to leave, when I stood, crossed the room, and reached behind the couch.

I pulled out the framed painting from the Bywater gallery. The one she had stopped to admire just a little too long.

Her entire body stilled, and her breath hitched.

I held it out. "I bought this for you."

Elizabeth blinked, looking up at me, still trying to maintain that professional distance. "That wasn't part of the plan."

I stepped closer, holding her gaze. "Neither are you."

She didn't move. Didn't speak.

"It's yours," I said softly, placing it in her hands.

Her fingers curled around the frame, but she didn't even glance at the painting. Her eyes were still on me.

"Why would you do that?"

I could have deflected. Could have turned it into a joke, shrugged it off, and made it seem like nothing.

But I didn't. Instead, I leaned against the wall, exhaling slowly. "Because I get it." My voice was quieter now. "Feeling like you can't have what you want."

Her breath caught. For a second, she didn't move. Didn't breathe.

I took a step closer. "Elizabeth—"

She shook her head sharply. "No."

I hesitated. "I think you—"

"Don't say it."

Her voice was barely above a whisper, but it carried more weight than a shout. Her fingers tightened around the frame of the painting like it was the only thing keeping her grounded.

I searched her face, looking for a crack in her resolve, some sign that I wasn't the only one feeling this.

"Elizabeth." My voice was softer now, careful, deliberate. "You know it too."

Her lips parted, like she wanted to argue, like she was about to deny it. But she didn't. Instead, she turned away, her shoulders tense. "Good night, Logan."

And then she was walking out, leaving me standing there with all the words I wasn't allowed to say.

Fine. She wasn't ready to hear it. Then, I wouldn't say it. Yet.

I listened to her heels clicking against the hardwood, listened until the sound disappeared.

Then I turned back to the piano, pressing my fingers to the keys.

The same melody.

The one that hadn't been there before she was.

# 17

## ELIZABETH

THERE WERE plenty of things I was prepared for tonight.

Logan showing up looking ridiculously good in a tux? That was expected.

Sophie dazzling the cameras in a dress that probably cost more than my yearly salary? That was part of the plan.

But Logan, seeing me and looking like he'd taken a punch to the gut?

I was not prepared for that.

I had been scanning the ballroom of Logan's charity gala, making sure everything was running smoothly, when I felt it. The weight of Logan's stare.

I turned and locked eyes with him.

His steps slowed. His expression shifted. He looked stunned, thrown off, lingering a second too long. His gaze dragged over me, slow, deliberate, like he was trying to reconcile something in his head. It was as if he wasn't expecting to see me like this.

I swallowed.

And then, as if remembering where he was, Logan blinked and turned away, his jaw tightening.

Right. I stepped back, tucking myself into the shadows as Logan and Sophie moved beneath the glittering chandeliers.

I wasn't even trying to be seen. That wasn't my job. I was here to manage things from the background, to make sure Logan and Sophie's entrance was flawless, to keep the press focused on their perfect, high-profile relationship.

But I still had to look presentable.

So I'd chosen a sleek, off-the-shoulder black gown, the kind that was classic enough to blend into the background but still made me feel like I belonged in a room like this. My hair was pinned back, a few loose strands framing my face. Simple. Elegant. Professional.

But Logan hadn't looked at me like I was blending into the background.

Shaken by his gaze, I stepped out of the way, fading into the shadows of the grand ballroom as Logan and Sophie took their place beneath the glittering chandeliers. They were the picture of elegance. Logan wore a perfectly tailored black tux, Sophie wore silver satin, her arm linked effortlessly through his. Exactly how it was supposed to look.

But for some reason, I felt like I'd swallowed something too warm. I shook it off, redirecting my focus to the stage where Logan would be performing soon. That was what mattered. Not whatever his look had been.

It wasn't the first time I'd noticed how ridiculously handsome he was. I didn't know what was happening between us. I mean, I thought of the very generous painting he bought me, and I felt like a live wire was humming under my skin.

Inside, I was in complete turmoil. Every nerve was firing, my heart kicking in my chest, my pulse way too unsteady for something that wasn't supposed to be happening at all.

I needed to shake this off.

Then, the emcee took the stage, microphone in hand. "We have a very special performance for you tonight. He's a multi-platinum artist, a chart-topping legend, and if we're lucky, maybe he'll even behave himself for the next three songs. Logan Richards!"

Applause roared through the audience as Logan took his place on the stage. I watched how tall and confident he looked. I crossed my arms, exhaling. How was I going to get through this? It must have been evident to every person in this room that I had a crush on Logan.

And then Logan looked at me.

Like he knew exactly what I was thinking.

Like he knew I was standing here, trying to hold myself together while everything inside me was unraveling.

Finally, he spoke. "First, I just wanna thank everyone for coming out tonight. It means a lot, not just to me, but to the real stars of the show—the dogs." A wave of laughter moved through the room, and he chuckled. "If you told me a year ago that I'd be here at a fancy gala raising money for an animal shelter, I probably wouldn't have believed you. But then I met Buttons."

Another titter of laughter, softer this time.

His voice dropped a little, taking on that quiet sincerity that had a way of making people lean in. "I came to New Orleans thinking I'd just be passing through, but... turns out, this city has a way of getting under your skin. The people, the energy..." He let out a breath, shaking his head slightly. "And yeah, maybe *someone* in particular had a little something to do with that."

He played his guitar for the first couple of songs. Crowd-pleasers. Familiar hits. The ones that had people swaying, smiling, mouthing along to the lyrics.

I let myself relax, just a fraction.

Then, he took his place at the piano, and everything changed.

"This next one," he said, voice easy, almost casual, "is something I've been working on. It's about someone who's become important to me."

A murmur rippled through the crowd.

Logan smirked. "It's not finished yet. But sometimes, a song feels right before you even figure out what it's supposed to be."

Logan let the moment breathe, fingers drifting lazily over the piano keys before settling into a familiar melody. The one I'd heard him playing in the studio.

Logan's voice filled the ballroom, low and raw and a little rough around the edges in that way that made you feel every word.

> *This girl moves like a New Orleans summer,*
> *Warm when she wants to be,*
> *No mercy in the heat she's bringing.*
> *No chance of a gentle breeze,*
> *Her mind's a rolling thunder,*
> *Her words cut sharply and cleanly.*
> *You'll feel the spark before you see,*
> *The fire in between.*
> *She's got her walls, she's got her pride,*
> *Won't let just anyone inside.*
> *But if you're lucky, if you try,*
> *You might catch the truth she hides.*

I stopped breathing. The words were perfect. The song itself would stitch up his reputation. A long song to the love of his life. And he was singing it to Sophie in front of everyone.

But he wasn't singing it to her at all. Logan's fingers moved over the keys like it was second nature, but he wasn't looking at Sophie. His gaze was searching.

And when his eyes landed on me, I felt something slip in my chest, something I wasn't ready for. Before I could even process what was happening, the song ended, the final notes faded into the ballroom like a secret too big to be kept.

And then, chaos erupted.

Sophie let out a dramatic gasp, pressing a hand to her chest. "Oh. My. GAWD."

I blinked.

Logan barely had time to brace himself before Sophie, in her floor-length designer gown, launched herself at him, wrapping her arms around his neck.

The crowd erupted into cheers, cameras flashing as she grabbed his face and kissed him.

I forgot how to exist.

It was obvious to me—painfully, undeniably obvious—who that song had been about. And yet, here we were, the entire world believing they had witnessed the most romantic moment of the century.

I forced my expression to stay neutral.

Mick nudged me. "Wow. That was something. You're really good at your job, Elizabeth."

I exhaled. "Uh-huh."

Logan, still slightly stunned, gave Sophie a quick peck on the lips, his gaze flicking back to me for half a second too long.

I clenched my jaw.

Because no matter how ridiculous this entire thing was, no matter how absurd it was to watch Sophie take credit for a song that wasn't hers...

We all had to pretend.

At least the night had been a success. The event had gone off without a hitch. The press got their photos, the donors were pleased, and most importantly, we raised a substantial amount of money for the shelter. I should have been thrilled.

Instead, I threw myself into finishing the night. Coordinating with the event staff and avoiding Logan at all costs. Because if I looked at him and acknowledged what had happened on that stage, I wasn't sure I could keep pretending.

The ballroom emptied, guests filtering into their cars, umbrellas popping open as the first drops of rain speckled the pavement.

I changed into jeans and tennis shoes, and I kept moving, checking off every last detail until I was the only one left, other than the event staff. I double-checked press logistics to ensure everything was officially wrapped up. Then, I went outside just as thunder cracked overhead and rain hammered down in sheets, drenching the pavement outside the venue.

I muttered a curse, pulling out my phone to call an Uber.

Before I could, a familiar voice cut through the storm. "You need a ride?"

Logan had also changed clothes. Gone was the tux. Now, he wore a fitted black sweater that clung to his frame, the sleeves pushed up to reveal the strong lines of his forearms. His dark jeans were slightly damp from the rain, and on his feet were boots, the kind that looked expensive but were well-worn.

I hesitated. "Where's Sophie?"

"Already at the hotel." He leaned against the frame of the car like he had all the time in the world. "I came back for you."

I cleared my throat, shaking off whatever weird static had settled between us tonight. "I'll be fine."

Logan gave me a look. The kind that said he wasn't buying a single word I was selling. He pulled open the passenger door.

I should have called an Uber, gone back to my own life, and kept pretending this wasn't happening.

But instead, I inhaled, ignored the way my pulse kicked up, and slid into the passenger seat.

The rain pounded against the windshield, blurring the street-lights into streaks of gold. Logan let out a low whistle, watching the streetlights flicker across the rain-slicked pavement. "Man... this place is amazing."

I glanced out the window. The French Quarter was different at night. Not the lively, crowded chaos of the daytime, but something slower. Like the city was finally exhaling after holding its breath all day.

I smiled, just a little. "Yeah. It is."

He tapped his fingers against the steering wheel. "I get why people fall in love with it."

I swallowed. So did I.

After a beat, Logan glanced at me. "So, why'd you leave?"

I frowned. "Leave what?"

"New Orleans."

I could dodge it. Change the subject. Spin some polished, professional answers that made my choices sound measured and strategic.

But I didn't want to lie to him. I let out a slow breath, watching the city blur past. "Because I had to."

Logan didn't push. Didn't fill the silence with empty words. He let me sit in it. Let me decide whether or not to go on.

I shifted in my seat, not sure why I was telling him any of this at all. "Jake had the support he needed here. I needed to build something for myself. I thought…" My voice trailed off. I bit the inside of my cheek. "I thought if I could create a career, make real money, and be successful, I could take care of him from a distance. The jobs I was qualified for paid so much more in New York. Even with the cost of living out there, it just made sense to base my career in Manhattan."

Logan exhaled, fingers tightening briefly around the wheel. "You feel guilty."

I let out a dry laugh. "That obvious?"

He smirked. "Only to someone who knows the feeling."

I turned my head, studying him. And for the first time, I wondered how much of his rebellion wasn't rebellion at all. How much of it was *running*? Running from the things he didn't want to face.

Something shifted in my chest, something I wasn't ready to name. So I forced a smile, tilted the conversation back to something familiar.

"I know I can be too controlling," I admitted. "I… I don't know. I guess I'm scared of losing people."

The words sat between us, fragile, like they might crack if I inspected them too closely.

Logan was quiet. And then, after a moment, soft, almost too soft for me to hear over the rain, he said, "You don't have to hold everything so tight, Elizabeth."

I turned away, staring out the window.

The downpour softened as we turned into the heart of the French Quarter. The streets glistened, lamplights reflecting off the wet pavement, turning everything into a soft, golden haze.

The city felt alive in a different way now. It was quieter and dreamier, like it had caught its breath after the storm.

Logan slowed the car to a stop. He didn't say anything at first, just stared out the window. Then, he exhaled and looked at me. It felt like the world went still.

"It's a beautiful night." His voice was lighter, like he was letting go of whatever had been weighing on him a few minutes ago. "You wanna take a walk?"

I should have said no. I should have kept pretending.

But I couldn't. Not anymore.

I turned to him, pulse steady but too loud in my ears. "I'd like that."

I stepped out into the night, and as we started walking, one thought settled in my chest with a quiet certainty.

I'd go anywhere with him.

And I couldn't deny anymore how much I liked him.

# 18

## LOGAN

THE STREETS WERE QUIET. Still damp from the rain, the pavement glowed under the soft flicker of gas lamps. Everything smelled fresh, like jasmine and wet stone, the air steamy with the lingering warmth of the day.

Elizabeth walked beside me, our shoulders brushing every so often, enough to send a flicker of awareness through me each time.

Neither of us was in a hurry. Neither of us was saying much, either.

The silence wasn't uncomfortable. It wasn't tense or loaded with expectations.

I exhaled slowly, shoving my hands into my pockets. "You know, every time someone tells me what to do, it feels like my father's voice in my head."

Elizabeth glanced over at me, brow furrowing slightly.

I kept my gaze ahead. "Telling me I'm not good enough."

She didn't respond right away. She just waited. Let me say it at my own pace.

"My dad was... intense," I admitted, voice quieter now. "He was a perfectionist, and he was relentless. Nothing was ever good enough. If I thought I'd nailed a performance, he'd tell me what needed fixing. If I wrote a song, he'd find the one lyric that didn't work." I swallowed. "And if I ever messed up? That was proof. Proof that I wasn't serious enough. That I didn't deserve the name he gave me."

I didn't mean to say that much. Didn't mean to say any of it, really. But Elizabeth didn't judge or jump in with solutions. She just listened.

I let out a short breath, shaking my head. "I think that's why I push back so hard. Every time someone tries to rein me in, it feels like him. Even when it's not."

*Even when it's you.*

She was quiet for a moment before murmuring, "That sounds... exhausting."

I let out a low chuckle. "Yeah. Tell me about it."

She hesitated, then asked carefully, "And now? Why are you referring to him in the past tense?"

I flexed my jaw. I couldn't tell her the truth. Not yet. So I shrugged. "Now, I'm trying. To be better. To prove I'm not the mess everyone thinks I am."

She stopped walking. We had wandered into a small courtyard, tucked between old brick buildings, with a fountain bubbling softly in the center. A few string lights hung overhead, their glow reflecting off the wet pavement and casting everything in a golden hue.

Elizabeth studied me with a softer expression in her eyes. "Logan... I don't think you're a mess."

I huffed out a dry laugh, rubbing the back of my neck. "You sure about that?"

She crossed her arms. "You're not the only one who feels like they have something to prove."

I tilted my head, waiting.

She sighed, glancing down for a second before looking back up. "If I stop working, I'm afraid everything will fall apart. If I'm not in control, then who is?" She cleared her throat. "I don't know how to let go."

I stepped closer. She didn't move.

I spoke more softly now, like talking any louder might scare her off. "You don't always have to carry everything alone, you know."

Her eyes met mine. She exhaled. "And you don't have to keep proving yourself to people who never saw you in the first place."

Something in my chest tightened.

Before I could think better of it, and before either of us could talk ourselves out of it, she leaned in.

Her face tilted slightly, her breath warm against my skin. And then her lips met mine.

At first, it was tentative. Soft. Cautious. Like neither of us knew whether this was a mistake, or the only thing that had ever made sense.

But then I shifted closer, and suddenly, it wasn't tentative anymore. The kiss deepened, and every nerve in my body fired at once. She tasted like rain and something I couldn't name. Something I wanted more of. Her lips were soft, warm, pressing tentatively against mine, like she wasn't sure if this was real, if she could let herself sink into it. But when I tilted my head to deepen the kiss, she didn't pull away.

She pulled me in. Her fingers curled into my jacket, clutching at the fabric like she needed something to hold on to. My hands skimmed her waist, then settled there, feeling the slight hitch in her breath, the way her body pressed just a fraction closer to mine.

I had imagined kissing her before—of course I had—but nothing had prepared me for this. For the way she fit against me, the way her lips parted just enough for me to taste her, the slow drag of her mouth against mine that sent heat licking down my spine.

I angled my head, chasing the sensation, my pulse hammering in my throat. Her hands slid up, fingertips brushing my jaw, and a quiet sound escaped her—a soft, breathy sigh that nearly undid me.

More.

I needed more.

But just as my hand slid up her back, just as I was about to kiss her deeper, she froze.

And then, she pulled back. "This is a bad idea."

I let out a short, breathless laugh, still feeling the ghost of her lips against mine. "Feels like the best one I've had in a long time."

She swallowed, gaze dropping to my mouth like she was fighting with herself.

For a second, I thought she might kiss me again.

Instead, she took a step back. "I should go," she murmured, tucking a strand of hair behind her ear. "We both need to think about what this means... or doesn't mean."

I could have argued with her about it. Could have pushed, could have asked her not to overthink it.

But I nodded. "For the record?" My voice was quieter now. "I think it means something."

She didn't respond right away. Just looked at me for a beat too long, lips still parted, as if she wasn't sure what to say.

Then she pulled out her phone and called an Uber. When the car pulled up, she hesitated. I almost said something. Almost stopped her. But I let her climb inside. I watched as the car disappeared down the street. Then I pulled out my phone and sent her a text.

**Call me when you get home so I know you're safe.**

A few seconds later, my phone buzzed.

Elizabeth texted her response: **I will.**

I exhaled, staring at the message. The rain had stopped, but the air still felt electric.

Like something had shifted.

Like nothing was going to be the same after tonight.

# 19

## ELIZABETH

THE NIGHT of our first kiss, we ended up on the phone for hours.

It started as a quick check-in after I got home, like he'd asked me to. A simple text, **"I'm home safe."**

And before I knew it, we were on the phone and talking about childhood bedrooms and the songs he used to write in secret. He asked about my favorite books from my childhood. We debated whether peanut butter should be crunchy or smooth. I told him about my ridiculous high school job at a bakery where I once mixed up salt and sugar in a batch of muffins and nearly sickened the entire morning rush.

We talked about nothing. And somehow, it meant everything.

Neither of us wanted to end the call.

So now I was running on about three hours of sleep, but I wasn't even tired. I was deliriously, impossibly happy. And I had no idea what to do with that.

I found Logan exactly where I knew he'd be: sitting at the massive grand piano in his studio, idly pressing a few keys as I stepped inside.

He wasn't the same Logan I'd met weeks ago. That Logan had been reckless, quick to deflect, quick to push against any structure, any rules. But now? There was something steadier about him, something more intentional.

He was still Logan—still charming, still maddeningly good at getting under my skin—but I could see the change in the way he carried himself. He wasn't trying to be the rebel musician anymore. He wasn't trying to burn everything down before someone else could do it first. He was showing up for his music, for himself. For me.

"Good morning, sunshine," he said, his gaze sweeping over my face like he was committing me to memory.

My stomach flipped. "You sound way too awake for someone who was up until five."

"You make it sound like I'm the one who kept you up," he said, smirking. "It takes two to tango."

I rolled my eyes and crossed my arms. "I never stay up so late. I always focus on being ready, being present for work."

He tilted his head, considering me. "And yet, here you are. Still standing."

"Barely," I murmured.

He grinned, leaning back against the piano. "Worth it, though?" His voice was softer now. A little uncertain.

I hesitated for a second and then nodded.

The warmth in his eyes sent another ripple of something through me, something new and terrifying and exhilarating all at once.

But I couldn't think about that right now.

"I came to talk strategy," I said, clearing my throat. "Breakup strategy."

He let out a low chuckle. "You know, I think those are the two best words I've ever heard you say."

My stomach flipped again. "Your PR nightmare is officially not a nightmare anymore. Sophie's getting the role she wanted, your label just greenlit your next album exactly the way you want it, and my boss, Vanessa, who has never said a nice thing to me in her life, complimented my work this morning."

Logan let out a low whistle. "The devil herself gave you praise? I think that qualifies as a miracle."

"I'm still in shock. But this means we did it. We pulled it off. It's been great doing this in New Orleans rather than on one of the coasts. We had friendly press, not too much of it, and the city wrapped around us in this perfect way. We got just enough buzz, but it wasn't overwhelming."

Logan smiled slightly. "Yeah. I like being in New Orleans."

I hesitated, then added, "But it's been a lot for Sophie to stay out here, and I know she wants to get back to LA."

Logan nodded, exhaling. "Yeah. I figured."

"And you're close to finishing your album. The breakup plan is solid. We can start easing you and Sophie apart publicly, no damage done."

For a second, neither of us said anything.

This was supposed to be the moment we wrapped things up and tied it all in a neat little bow.

Logan and Sophie would go their separate ways; I would move on to my next PR crisis, and everything would return to normal.

Except I didn't want normal. Normal meant walking away. Normal meant pretending the last few weeks hadn't changed me, hadn't changed *us*.

And that felt all wrong.

I gripped the back of a chair for support. Because if I let myself be honest, I had to admit that I didn't just want the controlled, carefully managed version of Logan I'd built for the world to see.

I wanted *him*. The chaotic, frustrating, devastatingly charming man who had somehow, against all logic, worked his way under my skin.

He cleared his throat and then spoke, "This could be the end of our PR relationship, but it doesn't have to be..." He faltered, looking suddenly unsure.

I straightened. My throat suddenly went dry. "Doesn't have to be *what*?"

He swallowed visibly. "The end of... other things."

I felt that invisible pull between us, stronger than it had ever been.

Before I could dwell on it too much, my phone buzzed. I glanced at the screen to see a message from Jake. My breath caught.

"What's wrong?" Logan asked, instantly alert.

I shook my head, rereading the message, barely believing it. "Nothing. Everything's fine."

His brow furrowed slightly, but I was already unlocking my phone, my fingers trembling.

I looked up, unable to keep the excitement from my voice. "Jake got preliminarily approved for the trial. The one I told you about on the phone."

Logan's face softened. "The one you've been fighting for."

I nodded, my pulse racing. "With my help, he can do it. This was the primary reason I accepted the job at Vanessa's firm. The pay helped cover Jake's treatments. He has a government job with good insurance, but it didn't pay for everything, and I wanted him to have the best. At first, that was all it was about, but then I realized the connections I would have with this job, and I worked to ensure he got exactly what he needed. And now, it's happening."

Vanessa was ruthless, with expectations that were brutal, but she was the best. And if I wanted to be the best, too, I had to keep up. Working under her meant learning how to see ten steps ahead and never flinch.

If it hadn't been for Jake, I think I still would have ended up in PR. I'm good at it. But maybe I would've stayed closer to home, somewhere I could run things on my terms instead of answering to someone like Vanessa. Somewhere I didn't feel like I was constantly holding my breath. Waiting. Hoping.

And suddenly, the thing I had fought for was one step closer to being real.

Before I could even process it, Logan was on the move. He closed the space between us in two steps, his hands settling on my shoulders, steadying me.

"Elizabeth." His voice was low, serious. "You did this. *You* made this happen."

I exhaled, shaking my head. "I don't know how to—"

He cut me off. "Just feel it."

I looked up at him, into those steady blue eyes, and for the first time in a long time, I let myself do just that.

No planning. No controlling. Just *feeling.*

And let me tell you, it felt good.

I let out a breathless laugh, shaking my head. "This doesn't feel real."

"It is real," Logan murmured. "And you should let yourself celebrate it."

I smiled, a little overwhelmed, a little dazed.

He tucked a strand of hair behind my ear. "Sophie's in LA right now."

I blinked. "And?"

"And that means we have a little time to ourselves before we do the breakup." His voice had dropped just slightly, the words slower, more deliberate.

I coughed, suddenly aware of how close he was. Close enough that I could see the faint shadow of stubble along his jaw, the way his pulse ticked in his throat. Close enough that my pulse had started hammering in response.

I should have said something practical. I should have steered us back to business.

But I didn't. Because the way he was looking at me, like he was seeing straight through all my carefully built walls, made it impossible to think.

His gaze flickered to my lips, just for a second. A breathless, charged silence settled between us.

And then he leaned in.

I didn't move. I didn't stop him. I *wanted* this. I wanted *him.*

But just as I felt the warmth of his breath, just as anticipation curled low in my stomach—

"Logan, you got a sec?" Mick's voice rang out from the hallway.

Logan froze.

I jerked back so fast that I nearly lost my balance.

A muscle ticked in Logan's jaw as he exhaled sharply, shutting his eyes for half a second like he was mentally cursing the universe. Then he turned, his voice tight. "Yeah, Mick. Be there in a minute."

Mick's footsteps retreated down the hall.

Silence stretched between us again, but this time, it wasn't the same.

Logan's eyes found mine, still dark, still *wanting*.

I let out a shaky breath, running a hand through my hair. "So."

"So," he echoed, watching me closely.

I licked my lips, my voice steadier than I felt. "I guess we dodged a PR disaster."

His mouth twitched. "I think I'd survive. And it's just Mick. He knows the Sophie thing is fake. Would it be so bad if he knew... we were..." Another pause. Another slow, deliberate inhale from him. Then he tilted his head, considering me. "Come with me."

I blinked. "What?"

"Come with me. Let's get out of here until Sophie gets back. No work, no responsibilities. Just *us*."

I stared at him. "Logan, I don't take days off."

He smirked. "Yeah, I figured. But maybe it's time you did."

I opened my mouth, but nothing came out. Because the truth was, the idea of stepping away from it all—of stepping *toward* him—felt shockingly, overwhelmingly right.

And that terrified me. But it thrilled me, too.

I swallowed, then smiled. "Okay," I whispered.

Logan grinned, running a hand through his hair. "I thought I'd have to work harder to convince you."

"Consider it a moment of weakness."

He tilted his head. "Or maybe you just realized you like me."

I groaned. "I take it back. I'm going home."

"Too late. You already said yes." He smirked, but then his expression shifted, a little more serious, a little more certain. "I need to figure out what Mick wants, and then we can go."

I blinked. "Go where?"

"Somewhere I go when I like to escape."

Warmth curled in my stomach, and I could barely breathe. "And what exactly are we escaping from?"

Logan's gaze lingered on mine, quiet and knowing. "Everything that doesn't feel like *this*."

A shiver ran down my spine, and I knew that whatever *this* was, whatever it was turning into, I wasn't ready to walk away. I wasn't supposed to be here—not like *this*. I was supposed to be the one keeping a professional distance, keeping things in order, keeping Logan in check.

But I couldn't argue with the way I was feeling. This was no crush.

I was falling for him.

It didn't matter how impractical it was, how complicated things would get, or how many reasons I could come up with to stop myself. When Logan looked at me like that—like I truly mattered—I didn't want to stop.

"Go pack," he murmured, his voice softer now.

And for once in my life, I didn't argue.

# 20

## LOGAN

I HADN'T EXPECTED the look on her face to hit me like that.

When we reached the treehouse, nestled high in the canopy of a sprawling cypress swamp, Elizabeth's jaw dropped slightly. The wooden structure was both rustic and magical, with rope bridges connecting platforms and an expansive deck that overlooked the shimmering water below. Spanish moss draped from the trees, swaying gently in the warm breeze.

She stepped out of the car, eyes wide as she took it all in. "What is this place?"

"It's a little hideaway. I found it when I was trying to disappear for a while on a past trip to New Orleans. Thought you could use the same."

When we reached the top, the view took even my breath away. The treehouse felt like its own world, floating above the swamp, with nothing but the sound of birds and the occasional splash of water below. Elizabeth wandered to the edge of the deck, her hands brushing the wooden railing as she took it all in.

"It's peaceful." Her voice was softer than usual, as if she were afraid to disturb the stillness.

"Wait until you see the inside," I said, pushing open the

wooden door. The interior was cozy, with soft cushions, warm wooden tones, and floor-to-ceiling windows that let the light pour in.

Elizabeth glanced around, her shoulders relaxing. "You weren't kidding about getting away. I feel like we're so far from civilization."

I grinned. "Told you I knew a thing or two."

The first day was perfect. We started with coffee on the deck, drinking from mismatched mugs while we watched the cypress trees sway in the breeze. I tried to impress Elizabeth by confidently identifying a bird.

"That's a pelican," I said, nodding at the white bird perched on a tree branch.

Elizabeth turned slowly, blinking at me. "That's an egret."

"It *could* be a pelican."

"Logan."

I crossed my arms. "Well, you don't *know* it's not some rare swamp pelican."

She looked at me like she was considering pushing me off the deck. "I do. Because it's an egret."

"Agree to disagree," I murmured, taking another sip of coffee.

By midday, I brought out my guitar and played a song I'd been working on. It was raw and unfinished, but I didn't care.

"That's beautiful," Elizabeth said when I finished. "You never play anything like that in public."

"That's because the public doesn't deserve it," I teased, but the truth hung between us: I'd never felt comfortable sharing something so personal until now.

That night, we played Scrabble, and I *did not* cheat.

Elizabeth eyed my latest move and folded her arms. "'Zantle' is not a word."

"It *absolutely* is."

"What does it mean?"

I hesitated for half a second too long. "It's... an old pirate term for, uh, someone who hoards treasure."

Her brow lifted. "You just made that up."

"That's slander," I said, placing my tiles back in the bag before she could challenge them. "And I won't stand for it."

"You're *so* full of it."

"Agree to disagree."

She picked up a pillow and hit me with it.

The next day was even better. We woke up to soft sunlight streaming through the windows.

We spent the morning playing chess (she was awful at it, but mostly because she kept getting distracted and making up rules). Then, later, she sat at the old upright piano in the treehouse, plunking out a melody, looking up at me with wide eyes.

"I remember this from my childhood," she said.

"You played?"

"For, like, two minutes. Then my parents realized I had no talent and redirected me to something I was good at."

I sat beside her on the worn piano bench, close enough that our arms brushed. "Play what you remember."

She did, hesitantly at first, fingers uncertain against the keys, but then she relaxed into it, playing a soft, simple melody.

When she finished, I rested my hands on the keys beside hers, echoing the tune and adding a few extra chords.

Elizabeth leaned into me slightly. "That sounds better."

"You just needed some backup."

She looked at me then, and for a heartbeat, it felt like the world was holding its breath.

By the third day, I knew. I knew this wasn't just a break from reality. It wasn't just two people escaping the world for a while.

I was falling in love with her.

I think I already had.

That evening, as the sun dipped below the trees, I found myself saying something I hadn't planned to. "There's something I need to tell you."

Elizabeth looked up from where she was curled beside me on the deck. "Okay."

I gripped my wine glass a little tighter before setting it down. "I told you my dad is sick, but I didn't tell you what he has."

Her expression softened instantly. "Yeah."

I exhaled. "He has Alzheimer's."

The words sat between us, heavier than I'd expected. I'd never said them out loud like that.

"For a long time, I was angry. I blamed him for everything. For being cold, for pushing me too hard, for making me feel like nothing I did was good enough. And I carried that with me. Until one day, he didn't even know who I was anymore."

I felt my throat tighten. "I spent years trying to prove something to him. But now? He doesn't even remember my name." My voice was rougher now. "It's hard to stay mad at someone when they don't even know they should apologize."

Elizabeth's fingers tightened around mine. "That's why your behavior changed."

I blinked. "What?"

She studied me, like she was putting the last piece of a puzzle together. "That's why everything spiraled last year. Why you went out of control."

I opened my mouth to argue, but nothing came out.

She wasn't wrong. It had started around then, hadn't it? The fights with the label. The canceled tour. The reckless decisions that made headlines.

"I—" I exhaled sharply, leaning back against the railing, staring at the darkened trees below. "I guess. That's messed up, isn't it?"

Her lips parted, like she was searching for the right words. And then she just shook her head. "No. It's human."

Something inside me cracked.

Elizabeth didn't press. She just ran her thumb slowly over my hand.

And then, like the realization had been waiting just outside my reach, it hit me.

I had spent my entire life fighting against my father's expectations. Trying to prove I was good enough. Making sure he saw me. And then, suddenly, he didn't.

And if he wasn't watching, then why did I need to keep proving myself? I had spent so long bracing for his criticism, measuring every step against his impossible standards, that when his demands disappeared, so did the reason to hold myself together.

But then why had I stopped spiraling?

Why had I been fine these past few weeks? I hadn't felt that self-destructive pull in days. Not since...

My gaze snapped to Elizabeth.

It was her. She made me want to be better.

Not because I was trying to impress her, not because I was proving anything to anyone, but because, for the first time, being better actually felt like something I wanted. I stopped fighting *everything* because, for once, I had something worth fighting *for*.

She was still holding my hand. Still there, steady and unwavering.

And before I could think, before I could second-guess it, I leaned in.

Our first kiss had been perfect, but each one after that was even better.

Her fingers tangled in my hair, pulling me closer, like she'd been waiting for this just as much as I had. My hands slid to her waist, anchoring us together, and for a moment, I let myself forget everything outside of *this*.

The way she fit against me. The way her breath hitched when I deepened the kiss. The way she leaned into me, like she couldn't get close enough.

Every time our lips met, it was something new, something more. Like we were learning each other one touch at a time.

And I could have kissed her forever.

Then—

A loud *knock* at the door.

Elizabeth jerked back, eyes wide, breath still uneven.

I muttered a curse under my breath and pushed to my feet, throwing the door open.

A teenage boy stood there, out of breath, like he'd been running. "Sorry to bother you, Mr. Richards. I work at the convenience store down the road. A guy named Mick says you need to come back to town. You don't have service out here, but people are looking for you."

Elizabeth sat up straighter. "Looking for him?"

The kid nodded. "It's all over the news. You two are all over the news."

Elizabeth shot to her feet. "All over the news?" I felt her go still beside me. "We need to go."

We barely spoke as we packed up, throwing our things into the car.

We drove in silence, winding through the swamp roads until, finally, Elizabeth's phone buzzed with a flood of missed notifications.

She clicked on the first link.

And there it was.

**ROCK STAR'S NEW MYSTERY WOMAN: IS THIS THE END OF LOGAN AND SOPHIE?**

Below were the photos of Elizabeth and me in the French Quarter. Her hand on my arm, both of us mid-laugh, standing too close.

Her breath hitched. "Oh, this is bad."

"How bad?" I asked, gripping the wheel tighter.

She swallowed, scanning the article, her face turning pale. "We just need to get back to the city."

I didn't argue. But as I pressed down on the gas, all I could think about was what she'd do when we got back. Would she put that wall back up? Pretend this didn't happen?

Because now the whole world was watching.

And I wasn't sure if she would run...

Or if I was finally going to convince her to stay.

# 21

## ELIZABETH

I HAD BEEN in some brutal meetings before, but this one? This one felt like a firing squad.

"This is bad," Sophie's agent, Cynthia, said dramatically, waving a printed article like it was a court summons. "The studio is freaking out. They're talking about reevaluating the role."

Sophie gasped. "What?!"

Mick sighed and pinched the bridge of his nose like he was physically in pain just saying the words. "And Logan, the label is... not thrilled."

We were in a hotel conference room. Sophie and her agent had flown in for the meeting, and so had my boss, Vanessa. That's how seriously she was taking this. And every time she spoke, she commanded attention: "This isn't just 'not thrilled,' Logan. They're reconsidering your album."

My stomach turned not just because I needed Logan's career intact, not just because my job depended on it, but because I had done this.

I had let things go too far.

I exhaled sharply, choosing my words carefully. "The photos were a misunderstanding."

A beat of silence.

Logan's jaw tensed, his knuckles whitening against the table.

I turned to him, ducked my head so only he could see my lips as I drew a shaky breath. "I didn't mean it like that."

"Then what did you mean?" Logan asked, voice quiet.

I wanted to take the words back, but it was impossible. What was I supposed to say? I couldn't admit to this room of people how I felt about Logan.

Vanessa scoffed. "A misunderstanding? Oh, how wonderful! Let's call the press and explain that you two just tripped into each other's arms. I'm sure they'll immediately retract everything."

My stomach twisted. But before I could answer, Mick clapped his hands together, his tone all business. "Alright, enough. Damage control time. What's our best move?"

Sophie, still in a state of crisis, sat up suddenly. "Maybe... maybe Logan and I should post a photo together. You know, all happy and couple-y?"

Vanessa scoffed. "Oh, yes, a photo. That'll convince people that Logan isn't secretly in love with his publicist."

My face heated. "He's not in—"

"We need something bigger," Mick said, cutting through the chaos.

Cynthia nodded. "Something... unshakable."

There was a beat of silence before Sophie's stylist, a man who was clearly in it for a free trip to New Orleans and had been scrolling on his phone for most of the meeting, suddenly said, "They should get married."

The room exploded.

Sophie made an inhuman squeaking noise. Mick let out a strangled laugh. Vanessa inhaled sharply, already calculating the logistics.

My brain short-circuited.

Logan blinked. "I'm sorry, what?"

Vanessa snapped her fingers. "It's genius."

"No, it's not," Logan said. "It's the dumbest thing I've ever heard, and I've heard a lot of dumb things."

Vanessa leaned forward, her eyes sharp. "You two getting married erases everything. If you're engaged, it looks like you and Sophie were together the whole time. It would prove that the photos with Elizabeth meant nothing."

Nothing? I stiffened, clenching my fists under the table. The late-night phone calls and shared secrets. The new happiness blooming in my chest. Logan's special smile when he saw me, and how my knees melted when I saw him. All of it... nothing?

Sophie's eyes darted between us. "I mean... that's a solution. But do we need to get married? Do we need to go that far?"

"Yes," Vanessa, Mick, and Cynthia said in unison.

Logan exhaled sharply, rubbing a hand over his face. " I-I don't know, this feels a little insane."

Before I could even think, the words were out of my mouth. "What about just an engagement?"

The room quieted.

I shifted my weight. "We don't have to go all the way to marriage. An engagement is still enough to sell the story, and we wouldn't have to worry about, you know..." I gestured vaguely. "The actual lifelong commitment part."

Sophie brightened. "Oh, that's a good idea!"

But Cynthia shook her head. "No, no, no, this is too far gone. We need something stronger. Marriage."

"Elizabeth," Vanessa's voice cut through the noise, smooth as ever, but with an edge that made my spine go rigid.

The room went quiet.

I forced my voice to sound neutral. "Yes?"

She tilted her head, studying me as if I were an intern who'd just made a fatal mistake. "Step outside for a second, would you?"

The request was casual. Too casual.

Mick groaned. "Oh, for—Vanessa, just say it. Whatever it is, it can be said here."

Vanessa smiled, slowly and deliberately. "Mick, I want this to be private."

My stomach twisted.

Mick waved a dismissive hand. "Fine. But make it quick."

I pushed back my chair and stood, following Vanessa toward the door as casually as I could. The second I stepped into the hallway, Vanessa's voice snapped me to attention.

I clenched my jaw. "What do you want?"

Vanessa sighed dramatically, her hands on her hips. "Why do you always assume I'm about to ruin your life? I don't want to threaten you, Elizabeth."

I crossed my arms. "Yet here we are."

She smiled, flashing perfectly white teeth, like a shark that had just spotted blood.

"Well, since you mention it..." She leaned forward slightly, lowering her voice just enough to send a chill down my spine. "Jake's been accepted into that clinical trial. Fantastic news."

My stomach clenched. "I know."

"But," she drawled, idly checking her nails, "his participation isn't quite locked down yet." She glanced up, her smile just a little too sharp. "You wouldn't want anything to... shift, would you?"

The words landed like a blow. Vanessa had put me in touch with the doctor at Beth Israel in New York City, who was working with the doctor at Tulane who had gotten Jake into the study. The study. The one that could change everything for him.

My pulse hammered. "You can't—"

"Oh, don't be dramatic." Vanessa gave an exaggerated sigh. "No one's pulling him out yet. I'm just saying that sometimes... things change."

My throat felt tight.

Vanessa levelled her eyes at me. "You're a smart girl, Elizabeth. You know how this business works."

I wanted to scream, to call her bluff, but I couldn't because we both knew this wasn't a bluff. This was Vanessa reminding me that she held all the cards.

I could fight her. But Jake? Jake didn't deserve to be caught in the crossfire.

Vanessa sighed again, perfectly content, like she'd already won. "Alright, darling. Let's get that engagement rolling, shall we?"

I forced myself to take a steadying breath. Shoved every ounce of anger, every flicker of fear, deep down where no one could see it.

Then we walked back inside.

Logan was watching and waiting for me. I had never wanted to tell him the truth more.

But instead, I forced the words out, knowing they would seal my fate. "This is the best move." The words tasted like poison. "We should make the proposal big and emotional. Everything about it needs to be believable. We'll coordinate with the press. Make sure it's perfect."

Logan turned to me, looking almost nervous.

"Please," I said softly. And that was all it took.

Logan exhaled, then nodded. "Fine."

Sophie, ever the actress, clapped her hands together. "I guess we're doing this. We're getting married!"

My stomach twisted again.

Vanessa cleared her throat. "Now that that's settled, we need a public moment to announce it."

Mick hummed. "A grand proposal. Somewhere famous, somewhere public."

Sophie gasped. "What about Cafe du Monde? Oh! We could do the whole ring in the dessert thing and put it in a beignet!"

My brain still felt foggy, but I forced myself to focus. "And Logan should write a song for Sophie and sing it at the restaurant."

The room went silent.

Slowly, Logan met my eyes. "I should what?"

"You should write Sophie a love song and perform it when you propose," I said, grasping for anything that would make this look authentic.

"It'll be romantic!" Sophie chimed in. "Oh! What if you write something like your song 'Wildfire Love'?"

Logan groaned. "I regret that song every single day of my life."

Vanessa clapped her hands. "It's a good idea."

"I will not do it," Logan said.

I nodded. "Fine. If not a song, then we make the proposal big and emotional. Everything about it needs to be believable. We'll coordinate with the press. Make sure it's perfect."

Perfect. The word sounded hollow. I swallowed the lump in my throat.

"Great," Vanessa said, smoothing out her suit. "Then we're settled. Get it done."

I nodded. Because what else could I do?

I had spent weeks repairing Logan's reputation, controlling the narrative, and ensuring the world saw what they needed to see. I had done my job.

And in doing so, I had backed myself into a corner.

Because now, the only way to keep my job and secure everything I had fought for was to help Logan marry someone else.

I clenched my hands into fists. This was wrong. *All of it.*

But there was no way out.

## 22

# LOGAN

WHEN THE DOOR SLAMMED SHUT, leaving only Elizabeth and me in the meeting room, I felt like I could finally exhale. But the breath didn't come easily. It stuck somewhere in my chest, tangled up in everything I wanted to say but couldn't.

I swallowed hard. "So, to recap: I'm now supposed to propose, possibly get married, and be expected to sing a love song to a woman I'm not in love with."

Elizabeth didn't say anything right away. She was still standing near the conference table, arms wrapped around herself, eyes fixed on the floor like she couldn't bear to look at me.

Like this was just as unbearable for her.

My chest tightened. *Does this ruin us?*

The thought came fast and sharp, cutting through the chaos of my mind like a knife. All I could think about was how much I didn't care about the headlines, the press, or the fake engagement.

I only cared about her.

And now, I had no idea where we stood. We weren't precisely defined before, but at least there was something to work with. But a fake marriage? That felt like a door slamming shut between us.

I had everything I could ever want: the fame, the career, the world at my feet.

Everything except her.

I let out a breath and ran a hand through my hair. "Elizabeth, this is—"

"I know," she cut in, voice tight. She finally looked up, eyes filled with too many emotions for me to name. "If this fake engagement doesn't fool everybody. It's bad. For my job. For yours. If anyone finds out—"

"If anyone finds out that I fell for you," I interrupted, stepping closer, "then what?"

She swallowed hard but didn't step back.

I kept going. "Because I don't care about this engagement. I don't want to be with Sophie. I want—"

*You.*

I almost said it. I nearly let the word slip.

Elizabeth's breath hitched, and for a second, I swore she could hear it anyway. Everything I wasn't saying. Everything I wanted to say.

She pressed her lips together and shook her head. "Logan, if this gets out, it will ruin everything. Not just my career, not just yours. I have to do this for Jake. I built my whole career to make sure he got the best care, the best chance. I can't let that fall apart now."

Her voice wavered, and I hated that.

Because I understood. This wasn't just about ambition or reputation for her. It was about her brother. About making sure he had a future. And even though family had never meant much to me, I felt something settle in my chest, knowing how much it meant to her. She'd fight for it with everything she had.

And me? I was the guy threatening to undo it all.

I clenched my jaw. My pulse hammered against my ribs, frustration tightening in my chest. She had to give me something. Some answer, some kind of reassurance that I wasn't the only one barely holding it together.

"So what, then?" My voice came out rough, edged with something

I wasn't sure I wanted her to hear. "Now I'm in a fake relationship with Sophie and a real one with you that I have to keep a secret?"

She inhaled sharply. "It won't be easy."

It wasn't the answer I wanted. But it was the only one I needed. She wasn't saying we had to end this. She wasn't suggesting we put whatever *this* was on hold.

Relief loosened something in my chest, just enough for me to move. To step closer, closing the space between us, my voice dropping lower.

"Nothing about you has ever been easy."

That made her smile. She reached for my hand, lacing her fingers through mine like she needed something to hold onto. "You're worth it," she whispered.

My heart stuttered. Three words. That was all it took.

Something in my chest cracked open, and the panic that had been clawing at me, the feeling that everything was spiraling beyond my control, eased.

I brushed my thumb over her knuckles, grounding myself in her. "You're worth it too."

Elizabeth let out a shaky breath, like my words had settled something inside her the way hers had settled me. She pulled back just enough to meet my eyes, and her look was tender. "We'll figure this out," she whispered.

I swallowed hard, my hands still resting on her waist. "Yeah. We will."

I'd never been one for self-sacrifice. My entire life had been built on doing what I wanted, when I wanted, and making sure no one else dictated my path. But now? Now I was standing in a hotel conference room, agreeing to a lie that would trap me for months, all because the woman in front of me had asked me to.

And the worst part? I wasn't even mad about it. Not really.

Because Elizabeth was still holding onto my hand, still looking at me like I was something worth choosing, even in secret. And that meant more than I was willing to admit.

I still wasn't happy. I didn't like what I had to do, but I could handle it.

She had my heart in her hands, whether she knew it or not.

## 23

# ELIZABETH

THIS WAS HAPPENING FAST. Too fast.

One minute, I was in a tense meeting being told that Logan and Sophie's engagement was the only way to fix this PR disaster. The next, Logan was down on one knee in a perfectly staged moment involving fireworks, a gospel choir, and an engagement ring the size of a small country.

Thanks to me, the headlines were on the cover of every magazine:

**Rock Star's Whirlwind Engagement. Sophie's the One!**

**Logan's Past Loves (and the One Who Finally Tamed Him!)**

**Too Fast, Too Soon? Fans Are Shocked About the Surprise Proposal**

Yeah, *you and me both, fans.*

After much (too much) brainstorming with Sophie's PR team, we planned the proposal to take place on a riverboat on the Mississippi, where I timed the whole shebang to the second so that Logan could get down on one knee just as fireworks exploded over the New Orleans skyline.

The proposal itself involved a gospel choir hidden below deck that dramatically emerged mid-song, a ten-carat engagement ring that probably needed its own zip code, and a second-line parade that arrived on the dock just as Sophie said yes.

Sophie, of course, ate it all up.

Logan, on the other hand? Let's just say he wasn't exactly *glowing* with excitement.

And now, with the wedding venue (a historic mansion in the French Quarter) booked, florists and caterers fighting to be involved, and half of Hollywood on the guest list...

I was the one making it all happen.

Which was how I ended up wedding dress shopping with Sophie.

We had photographers capture the moment for posterity (and for the tabloids), but after that, it was just the two of us in a private suite of a bridal boutique, surrounded by an overwhelming amount of lace, silk, and tulle. Sophie was thriving in her element, twirling in front of mirrors, champagne flute in hand, basking in the attention of the doting bridal consultant.

Meanwhile, I was one good inhale away from having a full-blown existential crisis.

"Okay, thoughts on this one?" Sophie turned, holding a sleek, strapless gown against her chest.

I blinked. "It's very white."

Sophie laughed. "I'll take that as a yes."

I forced a smile. I could do this. Be supportive. Even if the bride got engaged during a fake proposal I staged. Even if the groom was my secret boyfriend.

Yeah. I was fine.

"I don't know how you do it, Elizabeth," Sophie said, slipping into another gown. "Seriously. You've been such a rock through all of this."

I gave her a tight smile. "Well, it's my job."

She beamed at me in the mirror. "Which is exactly why I want you standing up there with me. Elizabeth, will you be my maid of honor?"

I choked on my champagne.

"What?" I sputtered, dabbing at my lips with a napkin.

Sophie turned, clutching the dress to her chest. "You know how much I trust you. I mean, you're already planning the wedding. And imagine how good it'll look for the press! It'll show how close we are, how real this is."

I froze, but she kept going, oblivious.

"You'd be the perfect person to be by my side. I'd be so lucky to have you."

I forced a laugh that sounded only slightly unhinged. "Yeah. So lucky."

The PR part of my brain knew she was right. It was the perfect cover. No one would suspect I was in love with Logan if I were standing next to his bride in a matching chiffon dress, smiling for the cameras.

The human part of me, however, was screaming. I had no idea how I was supposed to stand at that altar, holding Sophie's bouquet, while the man I wanted was putting a ring on her finger.

And yet, I heard myself say, "Of course, I'd be honored." I swallowed the lump in my throat.

Sophie beamed, clapping her hands together. "Oh, this is going to be *perfect.*" But then, mid-twirl, something in her expression softened. She smoothed the fabric of her dress again, this time slower, more thoughtfully. Her voice was quieter when she said, "You know, sometimes the person you love isn't the person the world expects you to love."

I frowned. "What do you mean by that?"

Sophie let out a nervous laugh and waved a hand. "I don't know. I'm probably just, like, overwhelmed by all the wedding stuff. Ignore me."

My brain was still turning over her words when she turned back to the mirror, tilting her head. "But, like... imagine if a princess fell in love with a regular guy."

"A regular guy?"

She coughed. "Yeah. Like someone who works with his hands. A carpenter. Or, maybe a mechanic. Someone who builds things. Or fixes things. Who's always covered in grease, or sawdust, or—"

"Sophie." I held up a hand, my eyes narrowing.

She startled, then cleared her throat. "What? I'm just saying. That would be insane, right?" She laughed again, a little too high-pitched. "Could you *imagine*? The tabloids would lose their minds."

Oh, I was imagining. I was imagining very hard. She was spiraling. That much was obvious.

"Sophie," I said carefully, testing the waters. "Is there something you want to tell me?"

Her whole body went stiff. "Nope!" She turned back to the mirror so fast she nearly tripped over the train of her dress. "Nope, nope, nope! Just bridal brain! Too many flowers! Too many dresses! Too much champagne!"

I narrowed my eyes. But instead of focusing on that, I turned back to the logistics. "Speaking of wedding stuff, we should probably get the marriage paperwork started soon." I pulled out my phone. "You and Logan will need to go to the courthouse to—"

Before I could finish my sentence, Sophie dramatically collapsed onto the nearest chaise lounge. "I cannot do this," she groaned, throwing an arm over her face like a damsel in distress.

"Sophie," I said carefully, "did you just faint?"

She cracked one eye open. "Obviously. Do you have any idea how exhausting all of this is? The planning? The relentless need for perfection? I am wilting under the weight of this wedding, Elizabeth."

Oh, for the love of—

I pinched the bridge of my nose. "You are not wilting."

"I am!" she cried, sitting up dramatically. "I'll need a honeymoon from my honeymoon!"

I resisted the urge to shake some sense into her. "Okay, fine," I said, rubbing my temples. "Why don't we take a little break from planning?"

Sophie immediately perked up. "Ooooh, should we get mimosas?"

I squinted at her. "You almost fainted from exhaustion."

She waved a hand. "That was ten seconds ago. I'm better now."

I shook my head, but just then my phone buzzed, and I pulled it out of my pocket, hoping for a message from Logan.

And there it was. **See you soon**, and a single red heart.

I exhaled, warmth blooming in my chest. Things with him were good. Better than good. Logan brought real happiness into my life.

In the middle of all this madness, we still carved out stolen moments between press events, whispered phone calls late at night, his hand brushing against mine when no one was looking. It was reckless. It was risky. And it was the only thing keeping me sane.

And now? I was about to see him. I tucked my phone away, already reaching for my bag.

"Sophie," I said casually, "we should wrap this up."

She barely looked up from her dress selection. "No, no, I need to try on at least five more."

I resisted the urge to groan. "Right, but if you don't stop now, we're going to be late for your spray tan appointment."

She shot up, practically knocking over a mannequin in her haste. "Why didn't you say something sooner?! If I'm even five minutes late, they might have to bump me to the lower tier of bronzing, and I *refuse* to look like an undercooked biscuit."

I grabbed her bag and handed it to her, steering her toward the door. "We don't want that."

She nodded, serious. "A movie star must glow, Elizabeth. I can't be matte."

I bit my lip to keep from laughing. "That would be tragic."

Sophie rushed out the door, already texting her stylist in a panic.

Just before exiting, she stopped abruptly, glancing back at me with an almost wistful expression. "You know," she said, voice softer than before, "sometimes I think about what my life would be like if things had been different."

I blinked. "Different, how?"

She shook her head quickly, plastering on her signature megawatt smile. "Never mind! Must be the bridal brain talking again!"

I frowned, but before I could press further, she was already gone, the door swinging shut behind her. Something about her words stuck with me.

But I didn't have time to dwell on it. A slow smile spread across my face, pushing everything else aside.

I wasn't thinking about the wedding, the lies, or what came next.

Because I was going to see Logan.

## 24

# LOGAN

I HOPED the music would drown out my frustration.

I sat on the edge of the couch, guitar resting on my knee, fingers running over the strings in a mindless pattern. I tried to write, to play, to channel the chaos inside me into something productive. But every strum of the guitar felt hollow, every lyric forced.

I exhaled sharply, scrubbing a hand down my face. This wasn't working.

Nothing about this situation worked.

Except Elizabeth.

The knock at the door had me up and moving before I could think twice. And the second I opened it, the second I saw Elizabeth standing there, I felt it. That stupid, unshakable rush of happiness I had no business feeling.

She looked perfect. Effortlessly put together, even after what had to be a long day of dealing with my disaster of a fake engagement. Her hair was a little messy from the wind outside, and she smelled faintly like flowers.

"Hey," she said, stepping inside.

"Hey," I murmured, watching her as she dropped her bag on the table.

She was wearing that determined look, the one that meant she was about to tell me something I wouldn't like, but she was going to make it sound logical anyway.

"I'm going to be Sophie's maid of honor."

My jaw tensed. "What?"

"For the wedding," she clarified, like I needed the reminder of the ridiculous circus my life had become. "It makes sense, Logan. It keeps me close, keeps me in control of the narrative."

I let out a dry, humorless laugh. "Right. Because nothing says, 'this makes sense' like having my *real* girlfriend plan my fake wedding."

Silence.

I felt it before I saw it—the way her whole body went still, the way her lips parted slightly in surprise.

*Girlfriend.*

We'd never put labels on it.

I swallowed, suddenly unsure. "I mean—"

"Say it again," she interrupted softly, stepping closer.

I looked up at her, my heartbeat hammering. "You're my girlfriend," I said, firmer this time, testing the weight of it, letting the truth of it settle between us.

Her lips curled, just slightly, like she was trying to contain a smile. "I've never been someone's secret girlfriend before."

I stood and huffed out a quiet laugh, tugging her closer until there was barely an inch between us. "Yeah, well... I've never had a girlfriend before."

Elizabeth's eyebrows lifted, her lips curving in surprise. "Never?"

I shrugged, standing before her, my fingers instinctively finding the curve of her waist. "I mean, I've had relationships. Or whatever people called them. But not really." I hesitated, the words thick in my throat. "I've never—"

I didn't know how to say what I meant.

Because I'd had women in my life. Plenty of them. Beautiful women. Famous women. The kind of women who looked perfect beside me in photographs, who whispered empty promises in dark hotel rooms, who wanted the fantasy of Logan Richards but not the man underneath.

And for a long time, I thought that was all I needed, that it was easier that way. Simple, fleeting, never complicated. But none of the relationships ever felt real.

Elizabeth was real. She saw me in a way that made my chest ache. From the very beginning, she had challenged me, called me out, refused to let me coast on charm or reputation. She wasn't dazzled by the lights or the headlines. She wasn't impressed by the things I'd used to keep people at a distance.

And somehow, that only made me want her more.

Elizabeth's lips parted slightly, and for a second, she just looked at me, searching. Like she was seeing something in me I hadn't even realized was there.

Then, quietly, she said, "I've never done this before either."

I frowned. "What do you mean?"

Her fingers toyed with the hem of my shirt, a nervous habit. "I mean... I've never felt this way before."

Something inside me shifted at her words, a warmth spreading through my chest, curling around my ribs. I'd spent years keeping people at arm's length, convincing myself I didn't need more than temporary, surface-level connections. That I was better off that way.

But with Elizabeth, I wasn't guarded. I wasn't pretending.

I was just hers.

I swallowed hard, tilting my forehead against hers. "That's kind of a big deal."

She let out a soft, breathy laugh, her fingers drifting to the back of my neck, playing with the short hairs there. "Yeah. It is."

I turned my head, brushing a slow kiss against her temple. "Guess we're both in uncharted territory, then."

She nodded, pressing closer, her warmth grounding me in a way I didn't even realize I needed.

But then, just as easily as we'd fallen into something raw and honest, she shifted. Her body straightened, her fingers untangling from the back of my neck, and suddenly, the business side of Elizabeth was back in control.

"We have an iron-clad contract with Sophie," she said, stepping away just enough to pace in front of me. "Six months, Logan. That's all. By then, your album will be out, Sophie will be deep into shooting the movie, and we have every excuse lined up for why you two won't be seen together much after the wedding. You're so busy with the album, she's on location, the honeymoon is delayed—it all tracks."

I sat on the couch and watched her. She was already in motion, running through the details like this was just another job. Another campaign to execute.

And heaven help me, I loved her for it.

I loved that she was brilliant. That she was focused and relentless and utterly unaware of how beautiful she was when she was working through a problem.

I loved her mind as much as I loved her body. I loved the way she stayed so determined, even when her goal was breaking me a little bit.

She kept talking, lips moving with precision, mapping out our next steps, but I wasn't hearing a word of it.

Because all I could think about was how much I wanted her.

Not just for stolen moments. Not just in secret.

I wanted this.

Every part of her.

She turned back to me, hands on her hips. "It's airtight, Logan. The public will eat it up. By the time we stage the breakup, no one will question it."

I didn't answer right away. I just watched her, letting the weight of what she was saying settle between us.

Finally, I let out a humorless laugh. "You've thought of everything, haven't you?"

Her expression softened, just for a moment. "That's my job."

I exhaled slowly, dragging a hand down my face. "Yeah. And I hate that you have to do it."

Something flickered in her gaze, but before I could name it, she sat down beside me, resting a hand on my knee. "We'll get through this, Logan. You and me. Together."

I swallowed hard, staring at her, knowing she meant it.

Before I could second-guess it, before I could let myself think too much about what came next, I kissed her.

She gasped softly against my mouth, but she didn't hesitate. Didn't pull away. Her fingers curled into my shirt, holding on like she needed me as much as I needed her. I deepened the kiss just slightly, memorizing the feel of her, the warmth of her, the way she melted into me despite everything.

I didn't know how long we stood like that.

All I knew was that when we finally broke apart, her forehead rested against mine, our breaths uneven, and the world didn't feel so heavy anymore.

I wanted to believe her. I wanted to believe that we could get through this, that six months would pass, and we'd be free to be together. But what if we weren't? What if the lines blurred too much? What if the world believed in this fake marriage so much that there was no space left for our real relationship?

Then I shook off the thought, pushing it away because right now, in this moment, she was here.

And that was all that mattered.

# 25

## ELIZABETH

ONE DAY. That was all that stood between me and watching my boyfriend marry someone else—a sentence so horrifying it deserved ominous music and a *Dateline* special.

I couldn't think about that. I had to focus. Everything had to be perfect.

Because even after the vows, the photos, the over-the-top reception, he would still be *mine*. Just... married to someone else.

I sat in the middle of my hotel suite, surrounded by glowing laptop screens, open planners, and a sea of color-coded spreadsheets. My carefully curated workspace had morphed into chaos. There were half-drunk coffee cups, discarded sticky notes, and a wrinkled seating chart that had been revised so many times it was starting to look like a war plan. I had a clear strategy and a clear goal.

Because Logan was worth fighting for.

Not just the Logan that fans screamed for, the one with the effort-less charm and the voice that could make stadiums go silent. But the Logan who never let me walk on the street side of the sidewalk. Who noticed when I was cold before I did and always found a way to fix it —handing me his jacket, turning up the heat, pulling me closer. Who saw when my shoulders tensed and somehow always found an excuse to make me laugh, even if it was at his own expense.

If I could simply get through a wedding and six months of waiting, Logan and I wouldn't have to hide anymore. I just had to find a way to keep Sophie and Logan apart during those six months, which should be easy. She would be busy filming, he would be on tour, and I would be handling his PR. Which meant I would be wherever he was.

So there was no time for self-pity. I had a job to do.

Spreadsheets. Timelines. Guest lists. Seating charts.

I exhaled, rubbing my temples, but the numbers and names still swam in front of me. It wasn't just the sheer amount of information. It was the constant push and pull, the need to control every detail, the knowledge that if I let even one thing slip, everything could come crashing down.

If that happened, I wasn't just risking a PR disaster. I was risking everything I'd built, everything I'd sacrificed for: Jake's future, my career, my sanity.

And Sophie wasn't making it any easier.

Every day, Sophie's behavior became more erratic. More demanding. She was micromanaging every detail, throwing tantrums over things no one cared about but her.

The peonies might be too pink. The calligrapher's handwriting was too elegant (how that was a problem, I still didn't understand). The napkins were off-white instead of ivory, and apparently, *that* was a tragedy of Shakespearean proportions.

It wasn't just that she was being a diva. I'd dealt with plenty of divas. This was different.

It felt desperate. Like she was afraid of something.

But I couldn't focus on that. Not when my job, the thing that secured my brother's future, depended on making this wedding a flawless spectacle.

And then, there was the *other* issue.

We had hit a roadblock when applying for the marriage license. Sophie's birth certificate had been impossible to track down—something about missing records and a clerical error. For a terrifying moment, I thought we'd have to postpone everything. But Sophie had figured it out at the last minute, saying she had another form of ID that would work—a backup, just in case. And sure enough, it had been enough to get the paperwork through.

A deep, familiar chuckle cut through my spiraling thoughts.

I turned, and Logan was there. Leaning against the doorframe, watching me with that knowing smirk, dark hair mussed from running his hands through it too many times.

Man, I loved him.

The realization was so sharp, so visceral, it nearly knocked the air out of my lungs.

The worst part was that I had to keep pretending I didn't love him.

I forced a smile and gestured at the spreadsheets. "Just making sure Sophie's dream wedding doesn't collapse."

Logan pushed off the doorframe and walked over, placing his hands on the back of my chair and leaning in close. He hummed, brushing a kiss to my temple, his lips lingering just long enough to make my stomach flip. "Come on. You need a break."

I did. Man, I did.

But I shook my head, already anticipating the next crisis waiting in my inbox. "I can't. I still have three vendors to follow up with, press placements to finalize, and Sophie's PR team wants to go over the seating arrangement. Again."

He smiled, but I could see the flicker of something else beneath it. Something tired.

He was exhausted by this, by the lie, by the fact that we only got stolen moments between press releases and wedding plans.

I was exhausted, too.

But I had to keep going.

Logan let out a dramatic groan, flopping onto the couch like I'd just informed him he had to handwrite all the wedding invitations personally. "Elizabeth. No one cares where they sit. It's a dinner, not the United Nations."

"Tell that to Sophie," I muttered, rubbing my temples. "She's convinced that if the wrong person is within ten feet of the dessert table, the entire event will be ruined."

"She's one day away from marrying me. The event is already ruined."

I shot him a look. He grinned.

Before I could argue, Logan walked to me, grabbed my wrist, and gently tugged me toward him. "Come on," he coaxed, his voice warm, persuasive. "Just ten minutes. No spreadsheets, no emails, no people breathing down your neck."

He was unfairly good at persuasion. Or maybe I was just desperate for a moment where my entire life didn't feel like an impending disaster.

So I let myself relax, let him pull me onto the couch beside him. He kissed me, slow and deep, and for once, I didn't think about the wedding or the chaos or the press releases waiting for approval.

It was just us.

And then—

DING.

My phone vibrated on the table, shattering the moment. Logan grabbed it before I could, squinting at the screen.

"Oh, come on," he muttered. "Tell me this isn't real."

I snatched it from him, reading the text from Sophie's assistant:

**EMERGENCY! THE SWANS ARE LOOSE.**

I closed my eyes and took a slow, steady breath. "I have got to start drinking on the job."

Logan's lips twitched. "How many swans are we talking?"

"Twelve."

His brows shot up. "Twelve unaccounted-for swans?"

I pinched the bridge of my nose. "They're not unaccounted for. They're just...not where they should be."

"And where should they be?"

"At the venue. In the decorative pond. Being decorative."

Logan crossed his arms. "And where are they now?"

I scrolled frantically through my messages. "That's...unclear."

Because some idiot, probably a well-meaning assistant, had

apparently taken one look at the enclosure and thought, *Do swans really need to be penned up?*

They do. They very much do.

I pulled up my contacts and hit dial.

"Who are you calling?" Logan asked.

"My bird guy."

He blinked. "You have a bird guy?"

"Of course I have a bird guy." I paced as the line rang. "You think this is the first time a high-maintenance client has let exotic animals loose in a historic venue? Far from it. I need to be in control of every situation."

Greg, my longtime contact at the New Orleans Audubon Zoo, picked up with a groggy, "Elizabeth, it is ten o'clock at night."

"I need an emergency swan wrangler."

A heavy sigh. "I knew this wedding was going to be a nightmare."

"I'll make sure a giant check gets donated to the zoo," I said sweetly.

Silence. Then, a resigned, "I'll be there in twenty."

I hung up and turned to Logan. "Crisis averted."

Logan shook his head in disbelief. "You just fixed an *escaped swan* problem in under a minute."

I shrugged. "It's what I do."

His eyes softened as he pulled me close, pressing a kiss to my temple. "You're amazing."

Even with my mind preoccupied with logistics and damage control, he made me feel lighter.

His hand slid to my jaw, tilting my face up so I had no choice but to meet his gaze. "You know," he murmured, voice low and rough, "it's the night before my wedding. And the only thing keeping me sane is knowing that I don't have to spend it with the bride."

My heart thumped, my breath catching.

"I wish it were you," he continued softly.

For a second, I forgot how to breathe.

How was I supposed to focus on anything else when Logan Richards—the man the world saw as untouchable and larger than life—was standing in front of me, looking at me like *I* was the only thing that mattered?

My fingers curled into his shirt, holding on for balance. "It is me," I whispered, my voice barely there. "You know it is."

He exhaled sharply, pressing his forehead against mine, like he was grounding himself in me. "Then be with me. Forget everything else. Just be with me tonight."

I wanted to. Man, I wanted to.

But I still had a few last things to check, a few loose ends to tie up before I could let myself fall completely.

I pulled back just slightly, pressing a kiss to his lips. "I will. I just have to finish a few more things. I'll be right there."

His jaw tensed, just slightly, disappointment flickering across his face. But he nodded, his thumb brushing over my cheek. "I'll wait for you," he murmured.

Then, without another word, he stepped back, grabbed his guitar, and settled onto the couch. His fingers found the strings, plucking out something soft, something familiar.

A song I knew was for me.

And as his music filled the quiet space, I turned back to my laptop, determined to get through the last of my work because nothing mattered more than being with him. Now, so his touch could soothe my nerves. And every day after the end of this charade, so I could love him like he deserved.

It was nearly three in the morning when I finally finished the last email, rubbing my tired eyes as I closed my laptop with a sigh of relief.

"I did it," I mumbled, turning toward Logan, only to find him sprawled on the couch, fast asleep.

The guitar rested against his side, one arm draped over his stomach, his face relaxed in slumber.

My heart squeezed. I crossed the room quietly, kneeling beside the couch and brushing his hair back from his face. He didn't stir. He just let out a soft exhale, lips parting slightly.

I wanted to wake him. Wanted to crawl into that space beside him and let him pull me close, let him remind me why this was worth it.

Instead, I just sat there, staring at him. For the first time, it hit me that I wasn't just keeping this secret.

I was losing something too.

I was losing the moments when he looked at me like I was the only person in the room, the quiet, unguarded versions of him that no one else got to see. The way he said my name, like it was precious on his lips.

I was losing the chance to be his first choice, out in the open, without hesitation or pretense.

I wasn't just helping him navigate the lie—I was trapping myself in it. I was the one making sure the headlines remained perfect, so the world saw exactly what it was supposed to. And every time I helped stitch together the illusion, I unraveled a little more inside.

# 26

## LOGAN

It was my wedding day.

I was supposed to be grateful. In just a few hours, I'd be engaged in a legally binding publicity stunt that would fix everything. It would save my career and cause the press to sing my praises.

So why did it feel like I was walking to the gallows?

A sharp knock on the door yanked me out of my downward spiral.

"Open up," Mick barked. "You have to be vaguely presentable for the cameras in an hour, and we both know that's gonna take work."

I groaned but stood, dragging myself over to the door.

Mick strode in like he owned the place, which, let's be honest, he probably could have if he wanted to. The man was a walking lesson in aging like fine whiskey. He was broad-shouldered, effortlessly put together, the kind of handsome that got sharper with time. His tux was already on, but he hadn't bothered with perfection. His tie was loose, his top button undone, like he'd been in a black-and-white GQ photoshoot and walked straight into my disaster of a morning.

He eyed me for half a second, then shook his head. "You look like a man on his way to a root canal."

I scrubbed a hand down my face. "Yeah, well. That's about how I feel."

Mick sighed and sank onto the couch, stretching his arms behind his head like this was just another Tuesday. "Alright. Let's hear it."

"Hear what?"

"Whatever stupid reason you have for sitting here looking like you're about to fake your own death instead of just saying what we both know you're thinking."

I turned back to the window, the sight blurred by the weight pressing down on my chest, jaw tight.

Mick waited.

And waited.

Then, finally, I said, "It's Elizabeth."

Mick snorted. "No kidding."

I shot him a glare.

"What?" He held up his hands. "Dude, I'm not blind. I see the way you look at her in every meeting. Heck, I see the way *she* looks at you." He frowned. "But I didn't think it was... this bad."

I hesitated. Then finally, I said it. "I think I'm in love with her."

Mick blinked. Once. Twice. Like he needed to reset his brain. Then, slowly, he shook his head. "Well."

I stared at him. "That's it? 'Well?' I just told you I think I'm in love with Elizabeth Bailey."

Mick let out a short, disbelieving laugh, rubbing a hand down his face. "What do you want me to do? Fall out of my chair? Clutch my chest? Gasp?"

I scowled. "A little more shock would be nice."

Mick shook his head again, still looking at me like he was re-evaluating everything he thought he knew about the universe. "I guess I just didn't realize that you knew it."

I frowned. "What does that mean?"

"It means I've known you a long time, Logan. And I've seen you with a lot of women." He gestured vaguely. "And by *with*, I mean mostly *near*, because let's be honest, you don't do relationships."

I crossed my arms. "Thanks."

"My point is," he continued, ignoring me, "you already look at Elizabeth like she hangs the moon. But I didn't think you'd let yourself admit it. To yourself, let alone to me."

I swallowed hard, feeling like the ground had shifted slightly beneath me.

Mick huffed, shaking his head like he was still wrapping his brain around it. "So the question is... what are you gonna do about it?"

I dragged a hand through my hair. "I don't know."

Mick rolled his shoulders like he was preparing for battle. "Let's go through the options." His tone turned all business. "Option one: You put on that stupidly expensive tux, go down that aisle, marry a woman you don't love, and spend the next six months pretending you're living the dream while secretly pining for Elizabeth."

I clenched my jaw. Elizabeth and I had a plan. One that required patience. Discipline. We were supposed to play the game, let the optics do their job, and wait until the timing was right. I told myself I could do that. I told myself I could fake it long enough to make it real.

But lying never came easily to me. I wasn't built for pretending. I never had been. I was real. Messy. Unfiltered. I wore my wounds on my sleeve. It was the only way I knew how to breathe.

And yet, there I was. Putting on a mask. Telling the world a story I didn't believe in.

I was doing it for Elizabeth. That was the only reason I could stand it. But each day I spent smiling next to Sophie, each headline we carefully crafted, each photo op I endured, chipped away at something in me. And I didn't know how long I could keep at it before the resentment took root.

I exhaled. "Option one sounds terrible."

"It is. But hey, you'll have great photos."

I shot him a look.

Mick smirked. "Option two: You blow up the wedding right now, tank your career, and send Sophie into a spiral so dramatic, the tabloids will eat for months. You talk to Elizabeth. Right now. Before you make the biggest mistake of your life."

I swallowed hard. Because I already knew what she'd say.

She wasn't choosing *this*—she thought she had no other choice.

My chest tightened. "And if she tells me I have to go through with it?"

Mick didn't even hesitate. "Then she tells you to go through with it. But before she does, you need to make sure she knows exactly how you feel."

The words lodged in my throat, caught somewhere between what I wanted to say and what I knew would happen if I said it.

I rubbed the back of my neck. Elizabeth had spent her whole life making sure nothing slipped through the cracks. She had sacrificed too much and carried too much, and she wasn't going to drop it all just because I stood in front of her and told her I loved her.

And yet—

What if she didn't have to lose everything?

The thought struck me hard, breaking through all the doubt and all the fear.

I'd been so focused on how impossible this situation felt for *me*, but maybe I was missing the bigger picture. Perhaps this wasn't about whether I was willing to walk away from the charade. Maybe it was about whether *she* should have to walk away from everything *she'd* built. Because her stakes? They were heavier than mine. She wasn't just risking her name; she was risking her brother's health, her entire career, everything she'd clawed her way to the top to achieve.

So maybe this wasn't just about loving her. Maybe it was about showing up for her and carrying some of that weight, for once. Making sure *she* didn't have to be the one who gave everything up.

I had money. I had power. I had influence. And yeah, I didn't like using those things. I'd spent my whole life fighting against becoming the kind of person who throws his weight around.

But for her?

For Jake?

I'd burn the whole industry to the ground if it meant she didn't have to choose between love and family.

She was trying to protect me by pushing me away. But what if I could protect her, too? There had to be another way: a different connection, a different angle. I could call people, pull strings. I had to. I wasn't just going to stand at that altar and let her throw everything away because she thought she didn't have another option.

Mick crossed his arms, observing me. "Look, if you go to her and lay it all out, and she still tells you to marry Sophie? Fine. Then you do it. At least you'll know you didn't leave anything unsaid."

He hesitated, then added, voice softer, "But if you don't? If you stand at that altar without making sure she understands? You'll regret it for the rest of your life."

I let out a slow breath, my thoughts still spinning, still landing on the same answer.

Mick clapped me on the shoulder. "And for the love of all things holy, stop making me say sappy stuff."

I huffed a quiet laugh, shaking my head. "Thanks, Mick."

He waved a hand. "Yeah, yeah. Now go make an absolute mess of your life. But, you know, in a way that ends happily."

With that, he strode toward the door and disappeared into the hall, leaving nothing but silence and the sound of my pulse pounding in my ears.

Mick was right. I had to tell her. Not because I needed to say it, but because she deserved to hear it. Even if she still told me to go through with the wedding.

Even if it changed nothing.

If there was even a chance that she thought she had to do this alone, then I had already failed her.

And I wasn't about to fail her now.

# 27

## ELIZABETH

JAKE WAS IN. The trial was official. The paperwork was done. His spot was secured.

The words blurred in front of me, my hands shaking as I reread the message over and over, barely able to believe it.

A breath of relief rushed out of me, a laugh bubbling up before I could stop it. I pressed a hand over my mouth, overwhelmed by the weight of it all. After everything—after months of uncertainty, of stress, of holding my breath—he was in.

I needed to tell Logan.

Because he was the only person in the world that I had told exactly how much this meant—the waiting, the worrying, the desperate hope that had felt impossible until this moment.

I turned, scanning the crowd, already moving.

And then I saw him, making a beeline for me. I made eye contact and ducked into an empty room. He followed me.

Before I could think, before I could second-guess, we collided.

My hands fisted in his shirt, his arms wrapped around me, and I pulled him into an empty room, crushing my mouth against his.

Logan let out a low sound, deep in his throat, and then he was kissing me back—fast, desperate, like he needed this just as badly as I did.

His hands slid into my hair, anchoring me, keeping me right where I was.

As if I were the only thing keeping him steady. It was like I was the only thing that made sense. I could have stayed like that forever.

But forever wasn't an option. Not for us. Not yet.

I broke away just enough to press my forehead to his, my breath coming fast and uneven. "Jake's in."

Logan blinked, his hands still cradling my face. "What?"

"He's in the trial. It's official. The paperwork went through. He's locked in."

I felt the shift in his body, the tension unspooling from his shoulders, the tight coil of worry finally giving way. And then his arms tightened around me, crushing me to his chest, his lips brushing my temple like he couldn't stop himself.

"Perfect," he murmured. Then he pulled back, just enough to look at me. And his eyes—man, his eyes. Bright. Blazing. Determined. "Let's get out of here."

I froze. "What?"

"We don't have to go through with this." His voice was urgent now, the words tumbling out fast, fast, fast. "We don't have to have the wedding. Jake's spot is secure. It's done. We can walk away."

For a second, I almost said yes. Because this was it. The moment I had secretly, desperately wanted.

But as soon as the thought formed, so did the panic. Leaving wasn't simple. It wasn't just stepping out of this room and into some fairy tale where love fixed everything.

Logan had a label that expected an album. A brand tied to a squeaky-clean wedding.

And me?

I had built my life around the idea of control. Around being the person who could manage the chaos, who could put out fires before they burned everything down.

If I walked away from this wedding, I would be walking away from the reputation I had spent my entire life building.

Vanessa couldn't touch Jake anymore, but she could still ruin *me*. She could take my job, my future, and rip the ground out from under everything I had built. One word from her, and every contact, every journalist, every client I'd earned would disappear. She could make it so that no one returned my calls. So that no one trusted me again.

And that was the real fear.

I needed control. I *craved* it. After everything I'd lost—my parents, my sense of safety, the version of my life that felt predictable—control was how I kept going. It was my armor. My system. I followed the rules, I was diligent, and I did everything right; in return, I built something solid. I built myself into a success. And Vanessa? She was the only one who could pull that foundation out from under me with a single, well-placed email.

If I didn't have control... what did I have? Who was I, if I wasn't the woman who always held it together?

Logan didn't understand that. He never played by the rules. That wasn't how he survived. He'd always pushed against the system, while I learned how to master it. And when Jake was at risk, Logan played along for *me* because I had too much to lose.

But now? Jake was safe. The job was stable. The plan had worked.

And Logan was done pretending.

I could see it in his eyes, feel it in the growing space between our bodies. He didn't want to live inside the script anymore. He wanted something real. *Us.* Out in the open.

But real meant uncertain. Real meant letting go.

And I wasn't ready.

I was doing this for *him*, too. Because, like it or not, Logan's career was hanging by a thread, and he was too talented to let it all go up in flames. I couldn't watch him throw everything away. Not when I knew how to save it. Not when I could still protect us both.

I wrapped my arms around myself like that could hold me together, like it could stop the shaking in my hands that I didn't want him to see. My throat felt tight, my chest burning with the pressure of everything I couldn't say.

I forced myself to meet his eyes. "No," I said, barely recognizing my voice. "We can't."

Logan's brows furrowed, confusion flickering across his face before something darker settled there. "Elizabeth—"

"You have to go through with this," I said, sharper than I meant to. Because if I didn't say it quickly, I might not be able to say it at all. "For your career. For mine.

His hands curled into fists at his sides, like he was barely holding himself back. "You think I care about photo ops and magazine covers? You think this fake life matters more to me than what we have?"

He stepped closer, his voice rising. "You keep acting like I need this, like you're saving *me*. But I've been doing this for *you*. I've played the game. I've followed the rules. I've stood there and smiled while you pulled the strings—because I *knew* what you were risking, and I wanted to protect that. I wanted to protect *you*."

He shook his head, breath ragged. "But Jake's safe now. And you're still choosing this... this lie over *me*."

I wanted to reach for him. To take it back. To say something that would make all of this make sense. But the words got stuck behind the pressure in my chest, behind the fear that if I let one crack show, everything would come crumbling down.

He looked at me like he didn't recognize me anymore. Like he couldn't believe I was the one asking him to do this.

And maybe I couldn't believe it either.

His hands curled into fists at his sides, like he was physically keeping himself from saying something worse. "How am I supposed to get through this?" His voice was quiet, like he was talking more to himself than to me.

My heart twisted. Because I knew Logan. I *knew* him. I saw it in his eyes. He was going to do it.

He was going to walk down that aisle. Smile for the cameras. Say the vows. Play the part.

Because I asked him to.

"Just look at me," I whispered. "I'll be standing right there."

As if that would make any of this easier. As if watching him marry someone else wouldn't tear me apart.

Logan let out a low, humorless laugh. "Great." He shook his head, his jaw tight. "That's comforting." Then, without another word, he turned and walked toward the door.

And I let him go.

And even though this secret still bound us, this tangled mess we'd created, it felt like he had just walked out of my life forever.

Because this was it.

The moment he was about to marry someone else.

And I was the one telling him to do it.

# 28

## LOGAN

I ALWAYS THOUGHT that when I got married, it would be for love.

That was the one thing I was sure of. I could screw up everything else in my life—burn bridges, make reckless decisions, throw myself into chaos. But love? That was supposed to be real. Love was supposed to be the thing that grounded me.

And I had finally found it. Against all odds. With Elizabeth. Sharp-witted, stubborn, brilliant Elizabeth, who could command a boardroom full of executives and still look flawless doing it. The woman who called me on my crap, who never let me take the easy way out, who challenged me in ways no one else ever had.

And instead of standing next to her, making impossible promises and meaning every single one of them, I was standing in front of a crowd of people, about to marry a woman I wasn't in love with.

When we had talked before the wedding, I finally saw it. All of it. Elizabeth's fear. Her obsession with control. She could never be the one who makes a wrong choice.

I wasn't the safe choice. I wasn't a choice at all.

No one had ever fought for me. Not really. Not my father, who couldn't look me in the eye unless I was achieving something.

And not Elizabeth. She was fighting to control the situation. To solve the problem.

And I was the problem.

So when the music started and I walked to the altar, I wasn't hoping anymore. I wasn't praying she'd come to her senses or change her mind. I already knew she wouldn't.

Sophie looked stunning. Her dress was something straight out of a fairytale, all lace and intricate beading, her blonde hair swept back in soft waves. She was the perfect bride. Any man would be lucky to have her.

But the only woman I wanted was standing, not next to me, but in the front row in a perfectly tailored dress. To the rest of the world, she looked polished and unreadable. But I knew her too well not to see the tension in her shoulders, the tight set of her jaw. She was hanging on by a thread, holding herself together like always.

And I imagined, just for a second, that it was her walking toward me. That this was our wedding. That she'd let go—finally, *finally*—and chosen love over control, chosen *me* over fear.

I begged her in my mind. *Please don't do this. Just throw up your arms and stop the wedding. Throw your arms around me and show everyone. Show me.*

But she didn't move. Not an inch.

She stayed exactly where she was, perfectly still, perfectly composed. Watching.

Why not get married now? What did it matter? At least I'd still have my music. And Elizabeth wasn't going to stop the wedding. She had nothing to lose by choosing me except for a boss she hated and a life she didn't even seem to want.

But she gave *me* up instead.

And that was it—the final blow.

"Logan," the officiant prompted, waiting for my vow. I took a breath, heart hammering, ready to say the words.

I opened my mouth.

"I can't."

The words weren't mine.

They came from Sophie.

The entire room gasped as she took a step back, pressing a shaking hand to her forehead. She turned to me, her eyes wide, her voice trembling. "I can't do this."

The air in the room thickened, stuck in my throat, suffocating me.

"I can't," she repeated, more to herself now, like she had just come to terms with it. Then she lifted her chin, squared her shoulders, and dropped the bomb that blew the entire wedding apart. "Because I think I might still be married."

Then, before anyone could even process what she had said—

**BAM.**

The double doors burst open so hard they slammed against the walls.

"Sophie Ann, *no!*"

The voice was loud, desperate, thick with emotion, and it belonged to a man.

A very sweaty, wild-eyed, flannel-shirt-wearing man, sprinting down the aisle like this was a movie. It was a guy willing to fight for what he wanted.

"I won't let you get away!" the man shouted, breathless, eyes locked on Sophie. "I love you!"

The room gasped as one.

Then, chaos erupted.

Sophie let out a startled half-sob, half-laugh, one hand flying to her mouth. For a second, I thought she might collapse. Then she ran straight to him like this was the ending to the rom-com she'd always wanted.

The press in the back exploded into a frenzy, flashes bursting like fireworks. Guests gasped, whispered, and some even cheered. Mick muttered something about needing a drink.

And Sophie? She leapt into the man's arms full tilt, dress flying, veil twisting like a flag behind her. It should've looked ridiculous. However, it didn't. It looked... right.

I stood there, frozen. Trying to make sense of the fact that this was real. That I wasn't dreaming.

The man held Sophie like he didn't care that hundreds of people were watching, like she was the only thing in the room. He buried his face in her neck, his whole body shaking.

"Sophie Ann," he breathed, voice cracking. "Babe, I knew you didn't mean it. I knew you couldn't marry him."

Sophie cupped his face, beaming through her tears. "Lambert, I thought I'd lost you."

Mick groaned beside me. "I'm getting a migraine."

Sophie turned back to the room, radiant and completely unbothered by the scandal she had just detonated. She laced her fingers through Lambert's and lifted her chin.

"I'm so sorry, everyone," she said, eyes shining. "But I love this man, and I can't pretend anymore."

Then she pulled him into the kind of kiss that belonged on a soap opera.

Another wave of gasps. I think someone fainted.

And me? I turned my head to find Elizabeth. She was standing just a few feet away, looking as stunned as I felt.

And for a split second, my heart caught. *Please,* I thought. *Please, just let this be the moment. Just let her see it. Let her do what Sophie did. Let her choose me.*

Then I saw the flicker of emotion in her eyes. Just enough to hope.

She moved.

But not toward me. Not to stop the chaos or whisper my name or do anything remotely cinematic.

She moved like a machine. Precise. Automatic. Like she'd flipped a switch.

Her mask slid back into place. The emotion was gone. She stepped forward, grabbed one of Sophie's assistants, and started giving clipped, sharp instructions. PR mode activated.

Elizabeth wasn't coming to me. She was fixing things.

And that was the confirmation I didn't want, but that I needed.

She had just watched a woman walk away from everything—reputation, security, certainty—for the person she loved.

And Elizabeth? She was focused on *damage control*. Of course. The wedding was imploding, the headlines were already writing themselves, and Elizabeth wasn't running to me.

I watched her go, with her head high, shoulders back, like she hadn't just torn something open in me and walked away with the pieces. She was strong. Unshakable. A force of nature. And screw it, that's what I loved about her.

But she didn't love me enough to turn that force in my direction. She wouldn't put her full weight behind us. Behind what we had. And I wasn't doing that again. I already know how that story ended. I loved my dad more than he ever loved me. Spent years trying to earn something that should've been mine to begin with.

I wasn't chasing love that runs away.

Elizabeth let me get to the edge and never once fought for me. She hated mess. Hated unpredictability. Hated losing control.

And me? I'm all of that. All of the time.

So, no matter what she said, or how tightly she once held my hand or how softly she whispered my name, I was never the man she would choose.

She just couldn't love me enough to risk it.

# 29

## ELIZABETH

SOPHIE'S BOMBSHELL announcement was still echoing in my ears.

This was a full-blown PR disaster.

My publicist brain was already spinning, running through the list of things I needed to do: activate the crisis team, monitor media and social channels, demonstrate corrective action, plan for long-term repair. Salvage Logan's image, protect my own.

How had I missed that she had been married—or was still married? Obviously, it had slipped through because I was distracted and had only myself to blame for this disaster. But before I figured everything out, I needed to control the narrative.

Control was everything. Control was what I did best. That's why I headed out of the room to begin mitigating the damage. I needed to make a statement to the press.

But then a flash of clarity hit me that I couldn't ignore.

All of that damage control was important to me. But more important was *us*—me and Logan.

We no longer had to pretend. We didn't have to sneak around or lie. Now, with Sophie's charade blown to pieces, nothing was holding us back. I could finally tell him everything I'd been too scared to say. I loved him. I wanted him. And now, we could be together without all the lies.

Logan and I could finally be together for real.

Of course, I couldn't represent him anymore. This conflict of interest had gone on long enough. I'd have to start transitioning him to a new team. I had plenty of contacts, people I trusted, but I needed to ensure it was someone who cared about him, not just about his public persona.

The media would have a field day. There was no way to reframe Sophie's runaway bride moment as anything but a disaster, and the second anyone saw me with Logan, the narrative would spiral. I could already hear the headlines. I needed a plan. A way to soften the impact. Something that made it clear that I hadn't hijacked the whole wedding just to end up with the groom.

And then there was my job. My clients. My reputation. PR wasn't just my career—it was who I was. I had spent years clawing my way up, making a name for myself. Would this undo all of it?

No. I could manage this. I could make it work. I'd step back from Logan professionally, distance myself from Sophie's disaster, and make sure my job didn't vanish.

It would be hard, but I could figure it out. I always did.

I just needed to talk to Logan first.

I pushed through the crowd, ignoring the flashes of cameras, ignoring Sophie, who was being spun around by her husband, Lambert, like this was some rom-com finale.

My eyes were locked on him, Logan, stepping into the courtyard.

I reached him just as he stepped into the quiet night air and grabbed his hand, turning him toward me. "We're free. Now we can finally put all of this behind us. We can figure everything out. Together."

His fingers twitched against mine, but instead of squeezing back, he slowly pulled away.

The loss was instant and awful, like a door closing between us. My heart stuttered.

His jaw tightened, and it was clear that something was very wrong.

The excitement in my chest wavered. I had been so certain that this was what he wanted too. That he would grab my hand and pull me toward something real. But now, his silence was an answer I didn't know how to interpret.

"Logan?" I asked hesitantly. "Talk to me."

He exhaled sharply and stepped back, running a hand through his hair. "You're already thinking about how to fix everything, aren't you?"

I frowned. "Of course. This is what I do. But this isn't just about fixing things. It's about us."

"That's the problem, Elizabeth," he said, finally looking at me. And I didn't like what I saw in his eyes. It wasn't anger; it was exhaustion, as if I had drained him of something vital. "You were going to let me marry someone else."

The words sliced through me. The air around me felt thin, like I couldn't quite take in enough of it. I opened my mouth to argue, but he was right.

I had let it happen.

I had stood there, convincing him to go through with it, telling him it was the best move, that it was what we needed.

My heart started pounding too fast, something heavy sinking inside me. "I didn't want to," I said quickly, shaking my head. "I didn't know what else to do. You know how much pressure we were under. I was trying to protect your career."

He let out a dry, humorless laugh. "And in doing that, you ignored me." His voice wasn't loud, but it was sharp. "I told you I didn't want this. I told you I didn't want Sophie. I told you that you were the only one I wanted. And you wouldn't listen."

I blinked hard, trying to keep the tears from spilling. "I love you." The words came out choked, desperate. "I was just trying to hold everything together."

He let out a breath, shaking his head, his voice quieter now. "That's the thing, Elizabeth. You love the idea of fixing things, of having control over everything, more than you could ever love someone else."

My chest cracked open. His words kept coming, relentless and painfully accurate. "And it's not just me. It's everything. Your work. Your family. Have you even talked to your brother lately? Or have you been too busy trying to control everyone's lives?"

I sucked in a sharp breath. My hands were trembling now. He wasn't wrong. I was always fixing, always planning, always trying to control things so they didn't fall apart.

But in doing that, had I caused them to fall apart?

"I love you," he said, softer this time, like it physically hurt him to say the words. "But I can't keep doing this. I can't keep being part of this cycle where you're trying to fix everything while ignoring the one thing that matters most. Us."

I reached for him. "Logan, please. I can change. We can make this work. We can fix this."

But then he let out a quiet, bitter chuckle. "My dad spent my entire life trying to make me into who *he* thought I should be. Straighten up, play it safe, make him proud. I disappointed him constantly, just by being myself." His voice dropped, quiet and raw. "I don't want to live like that again. I don't want to be an eternal disappointment to you, too."

"Logan—"

"I don't want to be something you *control,* a project." He took another step back. "I want to be your partner."

The world felt like it had tilted, everything off-balance.

I opened my mouth, but nothing came out.

*Say something. Fix this. Do what you always do.*

But my mind was blank. And then, before I could say another word, before I could fix any of this, he turned and walked away.

I had lost him. The courtyard spun. My hands were still trembling, my lungs too tight, like I couldn't get enough air. I wanted to call him back to fix this.

To tell him what? That I loved him? That I was sorry? That I had spent so long gripping control of everything in my life that I hadn't realized I was strangling the only thing that mattered? I took a shaky step forward. Then another.

But my phone buzzed in my hand.

I looked down and saw the name on the screen: someone from Sophie's team. Someone needed me to fix this mess.

Fixing things—that was what I did. It was the only thing I had left.

I exhaled, my heart pounding, and answered. My voice barely worked at first, the words catching in my throat. I forced myself to breathe, to be steady, to find the version of me who didn't break.

Because if I broke down now, I'd never be able to put myself back together.

# 30

# LOGAN

IF I HAD TO GUESS, I'd say it was sometime around three in the afternoon.

Or three in the morning. Honestly, who could tell in this place? The blackout curtains had been drawn for so long that the edges were curled from the damp. The air smelled like old takeout and newer whiskey, and I hadn't looked at my phone in... days? Weeks? Time had melted into this slow, syrupy nothing—like the bass from a party next door that I wasn't invited to.

Not that I wanted to be at a party. Not that I wanted to be anywhere.

The funny part was that as far as the world knew, I was doing great.

Sophie's wedding blew up in spectacular, viral fashion, sure. But the press spun it like I was a poor, heartbroken guy, and fans couldn't get enough of my music. I didn't want to see the headlines.

**"Logan Richards: Left at the Altar, Now Climbing the Charts."**

**"Heartbreak Makes Hits."**

**"Why America Is Falling for Logan Richards."**

They ate it up. Every perfectly framed photo. Every clip of me looking sad but *noble*. Every edited soundbite Elizabeth hand-fed them. Because yeah, that's the part I hated: She gave them the story.

Well-placed comments. Strategic photos. Just enough silence to make it look tragic, artistic, and *sellable*.

I thought Elizabeth was different. I thought she saw me—the real me—and didn't need to fix me. But I'll never forget the look on her face after Sophie called off the wedding.

She didn't run to me like I imagined she would. She wasn't relieved, or happy, or ready for us to finally begin. She looked panicked. Like all she could think about was what had just gone wrong. Not what could finally go right.

And when she did that, it hadn't just felt like rejection. It felt like confirmation, like I'd always been too much for people to hold onto. Too chaotic. Too emotional. Too loud.

No one ever asked what I wanted. Not my dad, not the label. Not even me. I never asked, because I didn't believe I deserved it. And Elizabeth... she was supposed to be the one who saw past all that. But instead, she flinched. She hesitated. She didn't choose me.

Sure, she came after me eventually. But by then, the damage was done. I already knew that I wasn't what she wanted. Not really.

The whiskey bottle next to my bed was half empty. Or half full, depending on your level of denial. I grabbed it, took a swig, and immediately coughed because it was flat and warm and probably older than this spiral I'd fallen into. My stomach turned, but not enough to stop me from taking another pull.

There were notebooks everywhere. Crumpled pages. Scribbled-out lyrics. Metaphors that would've embarrassed me even in high school. Every time I tried to write something, it came out sounding like I was auditioning for a middle school slam poetry club.

Rhymes about love that stand the test of time. Stuff that *meant* something when I wrote it with her in mind. Now it just felt like noise.

I sat at the edge of the bed, guitar in my lap, fingers resting on the strings without pressure. It was like I'd forgotten how to play. Like the notes were afraid of me.

Or maybe I was afraid of them.

Somewhere beneath the pile of laundry and pizza boxes, my phone buzzed. I didn't even look. If it wasn't Mick or my manager or the label, it was probably a fan account tweeting about how "raw" my new heartbreak era was.

I wondered what they'd say if they saw me now—unshowered, unshaven, sitting in yesterday's hoodie with my guitar in my lap like it might remind me how to breathe.

I plucked one string. Then another.

A D chord. Sloppy. Weak. Still, it rang out.

The sound echoed in the room. Small. Honest. Real.

I closed my eyes and whispered her name, not because I expected her to hear it, but because I needed to remember what it felt like to say something true.

# 31

## ELIZABETH

VANESSA HADN'T FIRED me from the PR firm.

I thought she might. After Sophie blew up the wedding, after the headlines rolled in, after Logan walked off that altar with heartbreak in his eyes, I thought I'd come back to New York and find a security badge that didn't work and a meeting with HR on my calendar.

But no.

Vanessa kept me on. Of course she did. The PR spin I had orchestrated in under twenty-four hours had been, in her words, "ruthless and brilliant."

Clients ate it up. So did the media. Logan went from "left-at-the-altar" punchline to sympathetic heartthrob, and our firm got more buzz than it had in a year.

Vanessa even smiled when I walked into the office after returning from New Orleans. A real smile. Brief. Shark-like. "Nicely done. Though next time, let's try to keep the runaway ex out of the client deliverables, shall we?"

Then she turned back to her computer because she hadn't realized that my personal life had been detonated on national television.

And that was it. Back to work. Back to pretending it hadn't gutted me.

I had been drowning ever since.

My calendar was wall-to-wall meetings. My inbox refreshed faster than I could clear it.

On paper, I was killing it. In reality? I was exhausted. And brittle. And numb in ways I hadn't known a person could be.

The worst part was how easy it had become to pretend. A smile. A sharp comment in a pitch meeting. A new suit. Better lipstick. Everything glossy. No one saw the cracks unless I wanted them to be seen.

And I never wanted them to be seen.

It was nearly midnight when I got home one night. It was a month after the wedding-that-wasn't. The building was quiet.

I dropped my keys on the kitchen counter, kicked off my heels, and poured myself a glass of wine without turning on the lights. The apartment looked ready for a photo shoot. It was immaculate, perfectly arranged, and utterly lifeless. I used to crave that kind of perfection. Now it just felt like I was living in someone else's story.

I took the wine to the window and stared out at the skyline. The city looked exactly the way I had always wanted my life to feel—structured and brilliant.

I didn't feel either of those things. I felt tired and hollow.

However, if anyone asked, I'd still say I was fine. That everything was going according to plan. In the world's eyes, I'd won. I'd salvaged the disaster, saved the firm, kept my job, and earned a bonus. I had proven I could stay composed in the face of chaos.

But the truth? The truth was, I hadn't felt like myself since New Orleans.

After a few minutes, I set the wine glass down and walked to my bedroom. I wanted to do something other than stand still and fall apart.

I opened the top drawer of my nightstand, looking for Chapstick.

Instead, my hand brushed against something small. I pulled it out and froze.

A matchbook. From that little jazz bar in New Orleans. The one Logan had loved. The one where we'd ordered dirty martinis and he'd made me laugh so hard I snorted in front of a trumpet player.

I stared at it for a long time. Then I sat down on the edge of my bed and let myself remember the last time I had seen him.

The way he had looked at me. As if he were choosing me with his whole heart. Like he was terrified and brave all at once. And the way I hadn't chosen him back. Instead, I turned around and managed the damage. Contained the mess.

Because that was what I did, right? I held it together. I kept the plates spinning. I built something no one could tear down.

But sitting there in my pristine apartment, holding a matchbook from a city that had felt more like home than this place ever had, I couldn't ignore it anymore:

I was in control. I had everything I used to want.

And I was *miserable*.

I hadn't chosen love. I had chosen fear. And now I was living with it every single day.

# 32

## LOGAN

I DIDN'T KNOW what day it was. It could've been Tuesday. Or Sunday. Or something in between. Time had blurred into a long, gray smear of nothing.

I hadn't picked up my phone in days. I moved like I was under-water—slow, aimless. Eat something, maybe. Try to sleep, fail. Try again. Wake up feeling worse. Rinse, repeat.

The only time I felt anything was when I sat at the piano by the window. I didn't play anything, but just sitting there was a bit of a comfort, somehow.

Just then, a knock came. It was a hard rap.

I ignored it. Like I'd ignored everything else.

Then I heard the key turn, and the door opened. Mick stepped inside, holding a paper bag and a six-pack of beer. He didn't say anything at first. Just dropped the bag on the counter and surveyed the wreckage. A few empty bottles. A pile of takeout containers. The ghost of someone he used to know.

After a moment, he nodded toward the guitar in the corner. "Still not picking it up?"

"I don't have anything left to say," I muttered.

"You do. Just say the thing you haven't said yet," he said. "It's there, but you're just holding back."

I pushed the blanket off and sat up. "What do you want, Mick?"

"I want my friend back. The one who doesn't let rejection turn him into a ghost with a drinking problem."

My jaw clenched. "Don't."

"You're not just heartbroken, Logan," he said, voice lower now. "You're hiding."

I stood up. "What's the point? The one person I let in saw all of me and walked away."

Mick didn't flinch. "And now what? You punish yourself for trusting her?"

"No." I looked down. "I punish myself because I was stupid enough to believe she would want me."

He leaned in, voice steady. "You've spent your whole life proving your worth—to your dad, to everyone...and now to Elizabeth. But let me tell you that there are plenty of us who already think you're great. Maybe it's time you stopped trying to earn your value from the few who don't see it and just be yourself."

Something inside me clenched. I hated how easily he could say it, like I could just flip a switch and stop feeling like I was constantly chasing something I'd never catch.

Mick sighed, leaning back. "You know what I think?"

"No, but I bet you're gonna tell me."

He smirked. "I think you're mad at Elizabeth for the wrong reasons."

I scoffed. "She was willing to let me marry someone else."

"She made a mistake," Mick said bluntly. "But she believed in you when you didn't believe in yourself. She's the one who stuck around when you were being a nightmare. And it was more than a job for her —anyone could see that. That's someone who gives a darn."

I swallowed hard, looking away.

"She saw you, Logan," he went on. "Not perfectly. But she tried. She wanted you. Just... on her terms."

I scoffed. "That's messed up. Even I know you have to compromise. If she wanted me—"

"If *you* wanted her," Mick cut in, "you'd get out of here and do something about it. Or, if you wanted to get over her, you would."

"It's not that simple."

Mick raised an eyebrow. "Isn't it? The way you talk about Elizabeth's choices, it sounds pretty black and white when it's her making the decisions."

That shut me up. Then Mick walked over, grabbed the guitar, and shoved it into my hands.

I stared at it. Heavy. Familiar. Distant.

I sat down with the guitar in my lap, fingers hovering over the strings. I didn't strum. I just sat there with it, as if maybe if I held still long enough, it would remind me who I used to be.

Mick didn't say anything right away. Just watched me like he was trying to piece something together. Then: "You both knew it wasn't going to last."

I blinked. "What?"

"She wasn't going to let you stay married to Sophie forever, Logan. Come on. She just... wanted to finish the plan. Do the job. Keep the train on the tracks."

I let out a bitter laugh. "That's worse."

"You were about to blow your life up in the middle of the biggest spotlight of your career. She didn't want to make it worse. She thought she was doing the right thing."

"So did I," I whispered. "I thought she saw me. Like, *really* saw me. And maybe that's what broke me the most. I thought she saw all the mess and didn't flinch. Turns out she was just concerned about trying to clean it up."

Mick leaned forward. "I know you. The only way you'll feel better is to write a song. Write what you feel. Even if no one hears it but you."

My throat tightened. I wanted to argue. But he was right.

"You want to hate her for not choosing you?" he said. "I don't think that's what happened, but if you're convinced, at least don't let her take your voice away."

I didn't say anything. He stood and clapped a hand on my shoulder. "I'll be back tomorrow, and I hope to hear what you come up with."

He left. And for once, the silence didn't feel like it was trying to bury me.

I sat there for a while. Just breathing. I hadn't just lost her. I'd lost myself. And I was the only one who could pull me out.

My fingers found the strings. One chord. Then another. Rough. Hesitant.

But real.

It wasn't a song about her leaving. It was about what it meant to love her. The way she laughed when she wasn't thinking. It wasn't pretty. Or polished. But it was mine. I wasn't writing for the label. Or the press.

I was writing for myself.

And it didn't sound like heartbreak.

It sounded like coming back to life.

# 33

## ELIZABETH

THE SMELL of burnt coffee filled my tiny New York apartment. I glared at the offending coffee maker like it had personally betrayed me, but considering I'd been so distracted that I forgot to put water in it, I had no one to blame but myself.

I sighed and rubbed my temples.

This was my life now. I was barely functioning, drowning in work, and waiting for forgiveness from Logan. Ha. That was never coming.

My phone buzzed on the counter. Vanessa's name flashed across the screen. I groaned because I already knew that it was going to be another crisis, another fire to put out, another way for her to remind me that even with my big promotion, I was still just a glorified problem solver.

But before I could answer, a knock at the door interrupted me.

I frowned. No one knocked on my door in New York. I swung it open and nearly dropped my phone.

My brother grinned, leaning against the doorframe like he did this all the time. "Hey, sis."

I blinked. "You're in New York?"

"Yeah, wild concept, huh?" He smirked and then stepped aside. "Oh, and I brought someone."

My stomach flipped as a familiar figure stepped forward, beaming.

"Sarah?" My best friend, my New Orleans partner-in-crime, stood there, looking entirely too pleased with herself.

"Surprise!" she said, breezing past me into the apartment.

I turned back to Jake, who just shrugged. "Yeah, so... we're dating."

I gawked. "What?!"

Sarah laughed. "Okay, rude. At least pretend to be happy for us."

I floundered for a response, but all I could do was stare between them. "Since when?" I finally managed.

Jake rubbed the back of his neck. "Uh... a little after you left New Orleans."

I narrowed my eyes. "And neither of you told me?"

"We were going to!" Sarah said quickly. "But then you were busy, and Jake said you'd probably just schedule a Zoom meeting to discuss it."

I whipped around to Jake, who dared to look amused.

"Oh, come on," he said. "You did schedule my twenty-fifth birthday party like it was a quarterly shareholder meeting."

I groaned, rubbing my face. "I was trying to be efficient."

Jake walked past me into the kitchen, shaking his head. "Efficient. Right. That's one way to put it."

I shut the door and faced them, crossing my arms. "Okay. You're dating. You're here. What's this actually about?"

Jake exchanged a glance with Sarah, who took that as her cue to casually wander into my living room and start flipping through my mail.

Jake exhaled. "Elizabeth... you need to get your life together."

I scoffed. "Excuse me?"

"I mean it," he said, stepping closer. "You've been so busy fixing everything for everyone else that you've completely forgotten to live your own life."

I stiffened. "That's not true."

"Really?" Jake arched a brow. "When was the last time you did anything that wasn't work? When's the last time you did something just because you wanted to?"

"I—"

"And let's talk about Logan," he said.

My stomach dropped.

Jake shook his head. "You loved him. And you let him go because you were too scared to lose control."

"That's not—" I stopped myself, voice faltering.

I looked at Sarah for support, but she just raised an eyebrow, as if to say she agreed with Jake.

"I was doing what was best," I said, but it sounded weak even to me.

Jake exhaled. "For whom?"

The weight of his words pressed down on me. I had spent years making sure everything around me ran smoothly. Making sure Jake had opportunities, that my job was secure, and that Logan's career didn't fall apart.

And for what? I was exhausted. And alone. Before I could respond, my phone buzzed again. Sure enough, it was Vanessa.

Jake glanced at the screen. "Let me guess. Another work emergency? Yet another scandal with one of your clients that only you can handle?"

I swallowed, looking down at the text: **Fix this or you're fired.**

The words felt different now. I had spent my whole life believing that control was security. That if I just worked hard enough, planned well enough, handled everything just right, then I could keep the worst from happening.

But in chasing that illusion, I'd given up more than I ever realized. I'd said no to spontaneous trips to New Orleans, to friendships that didn't fit neatly into my calendar. I'd skipped birthdays, canceled dates, rescheduled real life in favor of the version I thought I could manage. I'd buried dreams that didn't lead to stable outcomes. I'd built a life around predictability and called it success.

And Logan.

Logan was the last thing I lost to my need for control. The biggest, brightest, most unexpected part of my life, and I pushed him away because he didn't fit the plan. Because he was messy, and loud, and honest. And real. Because I was afraid of what it meant to choose something I couldn't manage or measure.

Now I could see all the sacrifices for what they were. Not steps toward safety. Just evidence of all the life I hadn't lived.

Logan was gone.

And no matter how hard I worked, I couldn't fix that.

My phone buzzed again, and it was Vanessa calling.

I took a slow breath. Then, without overthinking it, I picked up my phone and hit the decline button.

Jake's eyebrows shot up. "Did you just hang up on your boss?"

"That wasn't smart," I said. "Vanessa didn't deserve that."

I dialed her number.

She picked up on the first ring. "Elizabeth, I need you to—"

"I quit."

When Vanessa finally spoke, her voice was tight. "Excuse me?"

"You heard me." I swallowed hard, adrenaline rushing through me. "I'm done."

Vanessa spluttered, launching into a tirade about "irresponsibility" and "career suicide" and "I made you what you are."

But I didn't hear any of it. Because for the first time in a long time, I wasn't listening.

I hung up. Then I turned to Jake, with a shaky exhale. My pulse was still racing. "Well. That was... terrifying."

Sarah grinned. "Proud of you."

Jake smirked. "So what's next?"

I opened my mouth. Then I shut it. Because for the first time in forever, I didn't know.

And for the first time in forever, that didn't scare me.

# 34

## LOGAN

THE STAGE LIGHTS WERE LOW. Just a single warm spotlight, one mic, and an old acoustic guitar. No fog machines. No backup vocals. No drama. Except for the song I was about to sing.

My palms were sweating. Not from nerves. Not exactly. It was the kind of anxiety that lived in your chest when you were about to do something honest.

I sat down on the stool, took a breath, and started playing. It was the song I'd written about Elizabeth, and as soon as I finished writing it, I could tell that it was the best thing I'd ever written. And I wanted —no, needed—to share it with the world.

So that's where I was on that evening in Los Angeles. It was a surprise that I showed up at the club, but I kept it quiet because I didn't want a lot of fanfare; I just needed to get the song out.

I didn't look at the crowd because I didn't need to. This wasn't about them.

By the time I finished, the room was dead silent. Then the clapping started. At first, it was slow, then it built, and then the applause was thunderous. I stood, nodded once, and walked off stage like I hadn't just ripped out my heart and set it to a four-chord progression.

Mick was waiting for me in the wings, grinning. "Congratulations," he said, clapping me on the shoulder. "You're back."

I gave him a weak smile and kept walking.

The song was online before I got home. One of the audience members had posted it. And it blew up from there.

The next day, Mick tossed me a bottle of water, as if it were champagne. "The Internet is obsessed."

I groaned. "Kill me."

Mick smirked. "Can't. This interview starts in ten minutes."

A production assistant was already fussing with the mic on my collar, threading the wire under my shirt, and trying not to jab me in the ribs. I shifted awkwardly in the chair, narrowly avoiding knocking over the lighting stand next to me. My phone buzzed in my hand—probably another headline or a message I didn't want to see.

Mick plucked the phone from my fingers before I could glance at the screen. "Hands-free, rock star. Focus."

That's how I ended up in front of a camera, sitting across from a pop culture journalist who looked like she'd been waiting her whole career for a headline-worthy meltdown.

She leaned in with a sympathetic smile and a voice as soft as the couch we were sitting on. "So, Logan," she purred, "was your new song about Sophie?"

"No," I said flatly.

She blinked, slightly thrown. "Oh... okay. So... someone else, then?"

"Doesn't matter. She left," I said, sharper than I meant to. "That's kind of her thing—walking away."

I hadn't planned to talk about Elizabeth. Not like that. But the moment her name was even hinted at, it was as if the dam broke, and everything poured out: hurt, resentment, betrayal.

Because I was still so angry. I was angry at her for not choosing me. For not stopping the wedding. For watching me walk toward a future without her and doing nothing.

So yeah, I said those things because I wanted her to hear them. I wanted her to feel what I'd felt.

However, it didn't make me feel better afterward. If anything, it made me feel worse.

I walked into a meeting with Mick after the interview. He handed me my phone. I looked down to see if I had any messages, but the phone was out of battery.

Mick popped a protein bar in his mouth. "Your Spotify plays are up six thousand percent," he said around a mouthful. "Also, just FYI, we've received about seventeen boxes of fan mail since the song went live. Heartbreak is a good look for you."

I groaned.

He flopped onto the couch across from me, scrolling through his phone. "Oh, and did you know Elizabeth quit her job?"

My head snapped up. "What?"

He nodded, as if it were just a side note. "Yup. Left that ice-cold firm. Moved to New Orleans. Started her own PR company. Apparently, she's already pulling in clients."

I stared at him, the noise around me suddenly very far away.

"Big clients," Mick said. "Purpose-driven nonprofits, local food startups, even arts festivals. She only works with clients who do good. No generic corporate fluff."

"So she's not with Vanessa's firm anymore, and she's choosy about her clients?"

"Exactly. She's earning a reputation as one of NOLA's go-to boutique firms." He looked up from his phone and studied my face. "You okay?"

"Yeah," I said quickly. "I'm fine."

But I wasn't. Because I'd gone on national television and criticized a woman who had finally, finally stopped letting fear run her life. I said there was no future for us, but now she was building something real, something new. And all I'd done was weaponize the worst version of her.

The fans could cheer. The numbers could climb. But none of it felt like a win.

# 35

## ELIZABETH

My New Orleans office still smelled like fresh paint. Sure, the floors were uneven, the chairs were mismatched, and the front door stuck when it rained. But it was mine. And somehow, against all odds, it was working.

We'd just signed our fifth client in three weeks. It was an independent bookstore that wanted help launching a city-wide reading initiative. Real people. Real stories. Real work. And best of all, I didn't have to sell my soul to land them.

My team was small, scrappy, and full of ideas. I was learning to be a better leader than Vanessa had ever been. Not by controlling every detail, but by trusting the people around me. Letting go of the need to manage every word, every outcome.

It was terrifying. And freeing. And good. I was building something here in New Orleans. Something real. Which is why, when I heard the whoop from the bullpen and the sound of my name being shouted over the din of keyboard clacks, I smiled instead of cringing.

"Elizabeth! You have to see this!"

I leaned back in my chair as Zoey, our youngest account manager, practically launched into my office with her laptop open.

"Look," she said breathlessly, turning it around. "It's Logan Richards singing his new song. He used to be your client, right?"

I froze for half a second. My smile stiffened, but I nodded. "Yeah, that's right."

She set the laptop down and hit play before I could change my mind.

The video started. No flash. No band. Just Logan, a guitar, and a mic. It was the Logan I knew. The first note hit, and my stomach twisted. And then he started to sing.

Every line was raw and honest. The kind of honesty you don't recover from easily.

I felt it like a bruise blooming across my chest.

Next to me, Zoey sighed. "Isn't he amazing?"

I couldn't answer. But she was right. He was amazing. Every word, every note, felt like it had been torn out of him. Like writing it had cost him something.

Then the bridge came. It was soft, stripped down, almost like a whisper:

*You don't have to keep the sky from falling—*
*It's not all on you this time.*
*Let the stars shift, let the plans slip—*
*You're already mine.*

I felt it before I even fully understood it—that catch in my throat, that ache behind my ribs. But then he hit the final chorus, and there was no hiding from it anymore:

*If you let me, I'll meet you in the quiet,*
*Where the world fades out of view.*
*I'll be the space where you can loosen*
*Everything you hold like truth.*
*I won't tame the fire that makes you burn—*
*I'll just burn beside you.*
*I don't want to change you.*

*I just want to choose you.*

I knew without a doubt that the song was about me.

Every lyric, every line, was a map of the parts of myself I tried hardest to hide. The parts he'd seen anyway. The parts he loved anyway.

He had written it as if it were a prayer. And I was the answer. The song was about everything we had been and everything we could've been if I had fought for him.

After Zoey left, I sat at my desk, blinking fast, fingers trembling as I reached for my phone. I typed: **I heard your new song. It was the most beautiful song I've ever heard. If you ever want to talk, I'd like that.**

My thumb hovered over send, and before I could overthink it, the text message was on its way to Logan.

Before long, before I even had time to think about what I had done by texting him, a new headline popped up in my notifications: *"Logan Richards Opens Up About His Viral Song and The Woman Who Left."*

It was an interview clip. Just a few seconds. Grainy, low-res. But clear enough.

The interviewer leaned in, all faux sympathy. "So... where is she now?"

And Logan didn't even blink. "She left. That's kind of her thing—walking away."

The words hung there, quiet and brutal. The interviewer blinked, clearly not expecting such honesty this early in the conversation. Then, she recovered and leaned in with a sly smile. "Let me speak for all women everywhere: her loss. What woman in her right mind would turn you down?"

Logan just gave a little smirk and looked away. "I used to ask myself that every day. She's probably in some glass office right now, fixing other people's lives instead of dealing with her own. That's her comfort zone. Control the narrative, avoid the feelings." He shrugged. "But the truth is that some people don't want love. Not really. They want safety. Distance. A version of you they can manage. And when they see the real thing—messy, unpredictable—they run." He looked at the camera then, directly, and I felt like he was looking into my eyes. "I'm done chasing people who run." He held the interviewer's gaze for a beat, then added, "If she's watching. Good. Let her run."

The interviewer shifted, curiosity flashing in her eyes. "What if she hears your new song and wants another chance?"

Logan's jaw tightened. His voice dropped, each word carefully measured. "I don't care anymore," he said evenly. "I've moved on. I don't want her back. We're done, for good."

Well, that was it. Final. The door slammed shut with no turning back.

The blood in my veins felt like ice, and my stomach hollowed out. I stared at the screen, heart pounding, wishing I could take back the text I had sent him. Given the timing of the interview, it was likely he had seen the text before he began speaking. Right before.

I let go of the hope, the part of me that still believed he might ever understand why I did what I did.

No, I hadn't acted as I should have at the end of our relationship. I hated myself for that, but since then, I've left everything behind and tried to be brave. Tried to believe in new beginnings. But he was never going to forgive me.

My hands trembled as I opened his contact. I blocked his number. Not out of spite, but because I knew I wouldn't stop hoping otherwise.

I set my phone down gently, like that might soften the ache.

I would move on. I would forget him.

Even if it broke me in the process.

# 36

## LOGAN

THE GLASS DOORS of Elizabeth's new PR agency swung open as I stepped inside. For a split second, I considered turning around and disappearing into the French Quarter like a coward in sunglasses.

It was stupid to come here. Desperate.

But I was already in too deep.

The lobby was sleek and stylish. A group of well-dressed employees stood near the front desk, sipping iced lattes and radiating a cool demeanor.

The receptionist noticed me, blinked twice, clearly recognizing me, despite the sunglasses and baseball cap I wore. She dropped her pen, then scrambled to her feet. "Um. Hi. Can I help you?"

I gave her a sheepish smile. "Yeah. I'm here to see Elizabeth."

Her eyes tripled in size. "Elizabeth?" she echoed, as if it were a name she'd just learned for the first time. "And whom may I say is... I mean, do you, do you have an appointment?"

Behind her, a woman walked into the room, saw me, and audibly gasped. She clutched her chest and whispered, "Oh my gosh. Logan Richards."

Another woman followed, and mid-sip of her espresso, she did a double-take so intense she smacked directly into a ficus, apologized to it, and whispered a reverent, "Ow."

That's when I heard a voice behind me: "Okay, what are you all staring at?"

Elizabeth turned, and the moment her eyes landed on me, she froze.

Hair in a sleek ponytail, black blouse tucked into a tan pencil skirt. She looked even better than I remembered.

I thought about the text she had sent me—the one I hadn't seen until it was too late. The one that could've changed everything if I hadn't been too busy baring my soul on national television, completely unaware that she had reached out.

Elizabeth's expression was a mixture of surprise and guarded calm. "Hi." Her voice was steady. Too steady.

I coughed. "Can we talk?"

Silence.

She looked at me, and time slowed, as if we were in a movie, and she was deciding whether to forgive me or throw her iced coffee in my face. I swear, if I were told to leave in front of an audience of hyperventilating young publicists, I wasn't sure I'd recover.

I thought I was going to pass out. Or sweat through my shirt. Or both.

"Of course we can talk," she said finally, with all the calm of a woman who had absolutely no idea she was torturing me.

My lungs burned, and I exhaled. I needed to focus on breathing because I'd forgotten how.

The receptionist chirped, "Conference Room B is free. Would you like me to bring you coffee? Water? Whiskey? Me?"

Elizabeth gave her a small smile. "No, we're good."

Then she turned on her heel and walked toward the back, leaving me to follow while a half-dozen heads peeked over cubicle walls like meerkats.

Once we were in the room alone, door closed, she stood on the opposite side of the conference table from me, arms crossed, eyes steely. "What are you doing here?"

I cleared my throat. "I'm playing the Superdome tonight."

She rolled her eyes. "I mean, what are you doing *here*? Didn't you say that you were done chasing people who run?"

She was quoting my interview. I winced. "I didn't know you had texted me when I said that. I hadn't seen it yet. When I saw the text, I've been texting you and calling you ever since."

"I didn't know that," she said quietly. "I blocked you."

"Oh." My voice dropped. "Well, I read your text about a hundred times."

She didn't say anything.

"Please. I'm sorry I mentioned you to that interviewer. I was angry. Hurt. And stupid. But when I found out you quit your job.... I realized I'd gotten everything wrong."

She blinked, but didn't move. She wasn't going to make this easy on me.

I continued, "You left your job, something that gave you power and control. You gave up your safety net. That wasn't running away from me. That was risking everything."

She flinched, as if what I said had slipped past her defenses. But then the mask came back on.

I took a breath, trying not to push, even though everything in me wanted to reach for her. "When I was with you," I said quietly, "I was just me. Not the rock star. Just... me. And for the first time in my life, that felt like enough. I messed up. I know that. But if there's still even the smallest part of you that wonders what we could be, would you let me try again? Can we find our way back?"

Her eyes shimmered, but she didn't look away. Didn't run. I took that as a good sign.

Hope cracked through me like light through glass. I could almost see it: her hand reaching for mine, the two of us stepping into whatever this could be, letting everything else disappear.

But then she looked away, and the moment was gone. She shook her head slowly, and my heart dropped before she even opened her mouth.

"I can't," she said. Her voice was quiet, almost calm, but I could hear the crack just beneath it—the way it trembled like something trying not to break. "It hurt... Losing you. It hurt so much. But I did what I had to. I'm proud of what I've made. Proud of who I am now."

I wanted to reach for her. I didn't. "I'm proud of you, too," I said instead. And I meant it.

She blinked hard, and her jaw tightened like she was holding back something sharp. "But if I let myself fall for you again," she whispered, "and it doesn't work out this time... I won't come back from it. I *can't*. You have to let me go."

It felt like a thousand-pound weight dropped straight onto my chest, but I didn't try to argue. Didn't try to convince her. I just nodded.

"Okay," I said softly. "I understand." But I didn't. Not at all. Not even a little bit. I turned toward the door but paused in the doorway. Just long enough to say the one thing I hadn't said. "I've played to sold-out arenas. I've heard thousands of people scream my name every night like it meant something. Like *I* meant something. But none of it ever mattered the way you do."

My hand found the doorframe, steadying me. Something in me refused to let the silence be the last word. Not when the truth had finally started to crack its way out.

"I've written love songs for a living. I've made a career out of pretending I knew what it felt like. But you..." I turned my head slightly, just enough to catch the blur of her in my peripheral vision. "I mean, I've written love songs my whole life. But you're the one who made them true."

And then I stepped out into the bright glare of the office hallway, past a dozen eyes pretending not to see me, into fluorescent lights that felt too harsh, too indifferent to the weight of what had just broken behind me.

I just walked away. And I left my heart behind.

# 37

# ELIZABETH

SARAH AND JAKE took me out to dinner that night because they knew Logan was playing at the Superdome and didn't want me sitting at home alone, spiraling. When I arrived, they were already at the table, looking all lovey-dovey. I felt happy for them. If I couldn't be in love, at least my closest friend and my brother were.

Sarah gave me a big hug when I reached the table. With a gentle smile, she set a glass of red wine in front of me.

"We're here for you," she said, her voice warm and steady as she squeezed my shoulder.

Jake gave me a nod from across the table. "No pressure to talk about anything. But... you know. We're here."

"For emotional support," Sarah added, "and also pasta. Mostly pasta, if I'm being honest."

I smiled weakly and curled my fingers around the wineglass stem, more to keep my hands occupied than because I wanted a drink. I didn't want to talk about him, but I couldn't stop myself. I sighed, already tired from holding it all in. "So..." I glanced between them. "I saw him today."

Sarah's head snapped up. "Logan?"

Jake immediately leaned in. "How did that happen?"

"He came to my office," I said, trying to keep my voice even.

Sarah blinked. "He *what*?"

Jake frowned. "Like... unannounced?"

I nodded. "Yup. Just showed up."

"And?" Sarah prompted, narrowing her eyes.

"He asked me to get back together," I said.

That shut them up. Jake froze mid-sip. Sarah's jaw dropped. They stared at me for a long beat.

"What did you say?" they finally asked in unison.

"I said no."

Jake exhaled and gave a firm nod. "Smart."

"Very smart," Sarah agreed. "Good boundaries. That's healthy."

Jake gestured with his beer. "You've been doing so well. No need to go backward."

"Exactly," Sarah said. "I mean, yeah, he's a rock star, but you're... you."

"I know," I said, forcing a smile. "I thought it was the right call."

But even as I said it, something in my chest twisted. That hollow, echoey feeling that comes when you try to convince yourself of something that you don't quite believe.

Jake leaned back, satisfied. "Well, good. I'm proud of you."

"Me too," Sarah said. "Seriously. That couldn't have been easy."

I looked at my two best friends, saying precisely what I thought I needed to hear. I should've felt better, but I didn't.

I looked down at the wine glass in my hand. "He said something, though."

Sarah tilted her head. "Like... *something* something?"

I hesitated. "He said he's played to sold-out arenas. Thousands of people screaming his name. But none of it ever mattered the way I did."

Their expressions wobbled.

Jake blinked. "Okay. That's poetic."

"Mhmm," Sarah said, eyes narrowing. "Go on."

I took a breath. "He said he's written love songs his whole life.

Made a career out of pretending he knew what love felt like." I paused.

Jake waited. Then couldn't wait any longer. "...And?"

I looked up. "But I'm the one who made the love songs true."

There was silence.

Sarah slowly set her fork down. "Wait. Logan said that *about you?*"

I nodded.

Jake sat back, as if reprocessing the entire conversation. "That's not *nothing.* That's album dedication material."

"And I said no." The words felt heavier now. "I said no, and I just stood there and watched him leave." It sounded noble earlier. Now it just sounded empty.

Sarah was still staring at me, but now she looked like she was trying to see if I was joking.

Jake blinked slowly. "I mean... in *context,* that's a compelling monologue."

Sarah murmured, "Like, if someone said that to me, I'd like it."

I set down my wine. My heart was doing that tight, twisty thing again. "I made the wrong call, didn't I?"

Jake opened his mouth. Closed it. Then opened it again. "Yes. Yes, you did."

Sarah didn't hesitate. "One hundred percent."

I'd thought I'd stopped running when I left New York and came back to New Orleans. But the truth was, I'd only changed my zip code, not my patterns. I was still holding onto the biggest fear of all: fear of giving up my heart.

Well, no more. I wasn't about to let fear cost me the rest of the story. I sat up slowly. "I need to go get him, right?"

They both spoke at once: "*Of course.*"

I shot to my feet. "I need to get to the Superdome."

Sarah was already pulling out her phone. "I'm calling you a cab."

Jake shoved the breadbasket toward me. "You're going to need carbs for this mission."

I grabbed a piece of bread as if it were battle gear. "This is insane."

Sarah smiled. "It's romance. Of *course* it's insane."

Five minutes later, I was in the back seat of the cab. The driver—an older man in a Saints shirt and cap—turned down the jazz station just enough to glance at me through the rearview mirror.

"You alright, darlin'?"

"I need to get to the Superdome as quickly as possible," I said, already bouncing my leg like we were in the final round of a game show and the clock was running out. "Can you go any faster?" I asked, barely containing my desperation.

He chuckled, glancing at me through the rearview mirror. "Relax, darlin'. This is New Orleans. You gotta enjoy the ride."

"I don't want to enjoy the ride!" I nearly shouted. "I want to get to the Superdome."

"Now, now, don't be in such a rush," he said, turning *away* from the fastest route. "Have you ever taken the scenic way? Shows the city's soul."

"I *live here*," I snapped, gripping the seatbelt like a lifeline. "And I need to get there now."

"Oh, you're one of those *locals*," he teased, still driving like we were on a lazy Sunday drive.

I exhaled sharply. "I swear, I will give you a *massive* tip if you just drive like a *maniac* for the next five minutes."

He seemed to consider it. Then he nodded and finally hit the gas.

And drove me straight into the path of a second-line parade.

I practically screamed. "Are you KIDDING me?"

The driver grinned. "Ain't it beautiful?"

"No!" I slunk into my seat, fuming. Why had I been so blind? Why did I say no to Logan this morning? Now, I was going to miss him. I was going to *miss him,* and then what would I do?

He'd get on his tour bus. Or his tour plane. Or write a song called *'The One That Said No.'*

And I'd have to hear it in Walgreens for the rest of my life.

Nope. Not happening.

I was *not* going to be the girl who let the love of her life walk away. I threw the driver some money, jumped out of the cab, and hit the sidewalk running.

It was chaos. The street was a riot of brass instruments, parasols, sequins, and joy. The parade blocked the intersection, as if the universe had decided *this* was the moment to test my emotional endurance.

"Holy cannoli," I muttered, nearly tripping over a trumpet player in a gold suit, "if I miss him because of a parade—"

But it was too late. The music was too loud, the street too packed, and the dancers too committed to not letting me pass.

A woman looped a feather boa around my neck. "DANCE YOUR WAY THROUGH, BABY!" she yelled, thrusting a tambourine into my hands.

I wanted to scream. Or cry. Or turn back time and *not* say no to the man who wrote songs about me. What kind of idiot says no to that? Who does that?

Oh right. Me. I *did that.*

I was going to miss him. I was going to miss him, and I'd never get to say I was wrong. Never get to see the look on his face when I said *yes.*

I *had* to get to him.

So I did the only thing I could do.

I twirled.

Through the chaos, through the brass section, past two toddlers with maracas and a man wearing nothing but beads and a tutu, I tambourined my way across the street like a deranged Mardi Gras fairy with a broken heart and questionable decision-making skills.

Finally—breathless, glitter-streaked, and on the verge of tears—I emerged from the other side of the parade like I'd just been spit out by a sparkly hurricane.

This city was going to kill me.

But hopefully not before I found Logan.

By the time I reached the Superdome, I was breathless. I sprinted up to the front doors, lungs burning, hair sticking to my forehead, and chest heaving. The thump of bass pulsed through the walls as I skidded to a stop outside the Superdome, breathless and covered in parade glitter. I could hear the crowd roaring inside. The show was already more than halfway over.

I sprinted to the nearest entrance, straight into a very unimpressed security guard.

"Whoa there, ma'am," he said, holding out a hand. "I need to see your ticket. Do you have one?"

I hesitated. "Okay, technically... no."

He didn't blink. "Then *technically*... you're not getting in."

I groaned. "I need to see Logan Richards."

He raised an eyebrow. "Yeah, you and half of New Orleans. This show is sold out."

"No, I'm not here for the concert. I don't need a seat. I just need to talk to him. Like, immediately."

He crossed his arms. "And why would that be?"

I took a breath, straightened my spine, and tried to channel the tiniest sliver of dignity I had left. "To stop him from leaving the city before I can tell him that I'm in love with him."

He squinted. "You know how many women try that line on me?"

That was it. That was the moment I felt my hope start to crack.

I stood there, heart racing, glitter clinging to my hair, and realized how stupid I was. Of *course,* the guard wasn't going to let me in. Of *course,* I'd shown up too late. The show was more than halfway over, and soon Logan would be halfway back to his hotel suite or tour bus or *someone else.*

I turned away from the entrance, my chest tight and my throat burning. Maybe I deserved this. Maybe that's what happens when you say no to someone who says you make love songs true.

I wandered around the corner of the building, away from the crowds and the noise, toward the quiet loading area behind the Dome. I didn't even know where I was going, but I just knew I couldn't stand at that gate one second longer.

Just then, I spotted a familiar face near the backstage entrance.

"Mick!" I yelled, waving both arms like a stranded tourist flagging down a rescue boat.

He turned, took one look at me, with the boa and Mardi Gras

beads, and sighed like he'd just aged a decade. "You look like Mardi Gras exploded and then filed a restraining order."

I was too flustered to feel embarrassed. "I need to see Logan."

Mick muttered something under his breath, possibly a prayer, then fished a press pass out of his jacket. "This belonged to someone named Rachel. She was too emotionally stable to be here tonight."

"I love Rachel. Thank her for me."

"Don't make me regret this," he said, handing it over.

"You won't," I promised, throwing the pass around my neck and falling into step beside him.

As we slipped through a side corridor, the roar of the crowd rolled over me: loud, electric, and thrumming with adrenaline.

Mick slowed, turning to face me. "Hey."

I blinked. "Yeah?"

He reached out and tugged a feather out of my hair. "Go get our guy."

I smiled, nerves bubbling up again. But then he surprised me and pulled me into a quick, gruff hug before pulling back and squeezing my shoulder. "It's good to see you, kid."

I leaned up on impulse and kissed him on the cheek. "Thanks, Mick."

He waved me off like it was no big deal, but I saw the way his jaw tightened, just slightly. As he turned to head toward the crew area, he called out over his shoulder: "Don't screw it up."

I didn't plan to. Not this time.

I was tucked into a makeshift press section just off the side of the stage, close enough to feel the bass in my chest but far enough that no one would notice me hiding behind a row of folding chairs. I crouched low, scanning the massive stage through a blur of lights and nerves.

And there he was. Lit up in golden light, a guitar slung low on his hip, his voice echoing through the Superdome.

He looked beautiful. And heartbroken. And mine, if I wasn't too late.

"This next song is very special to me," he said into the mic, and the crowd quieted. "And this is the last time I'm going to sing it."

A few murmurs rose.

He continued. "Some songs just aren't meant for crowds, and this one hits a little too close to home. But tonight, I'll give it one last go."

And then came the first chord.

My song.

I knew it instantly. The opening note hit like muscle memory straight to the heart. My stomach flipped. My throat closed. I panicked. I had to do something.

Eyes scanning the arena like a lunatic on a mission, I spotted the tech booth. It was positioned about a hundred feet from the stage, just behind the sound pit and elevated on a platform so the crew had a clear line of sight. From up there, they could see everything: the lights, the screens, the band. I took off toward it, weaving my way through the people packed into the floor section.

When I got there, a crew member glanced up from a monitor. "Hey! What are you doing?"

"I'm fixing the flux capacitor," I said with full, fake authority, walking as if I had somewhere to be and that my badge permitted me to be there.

"The what?" He squinted. "Do you even *work* here?"

I approached the nearest panel of buttons and knobs as if NASA had trained me. "Yup. It's an emergency... uh... camera patch override. I've got this. You just keep doing what you're doing."

I had no plan. And little idea what most of the buttons did.

Before the crew member could figure out that I didn't belong there, I slammed my hand down on a red button.

There was a pause.

Then I heard someone gasp, somewhere out in the crowd.

I turned.

And saw my face.

*My actual face.*

Plastered across the Jumbotron.

# 38

## LOGAN

I WASN'T LYING when I said this would be the last time I sang this song.

It was too painful.

Every time I played the opening chords, it felt like reopening a wound that had never fully scabbed over. Like I was holding my heart up to the mic and asking it to bleed on cue, in front of thousands of strangers.

The lyrics came easily, not because I rehearsed them, but because they were etched into me, branded into every part of me that had once believed that Elizabeth loved me.

Elizabeth's name was never in the lyrics, but she was in every line.

And now that she'd said no, there was nothing left to wait for. No maybe. No second chance. Just silence.

So yeah, I was done. Done hoping. Done wondering. Done dragging this song—and my heart—into every arena like maybe this time, it would feel different.

This was the last time. The final chorus was rising, building beneath my fingers, my voice raw from everything I wasn't saying.

I closed my eyes.

And then a hush rippled through the crowd. I opened my eyes and looked up, and I froze. It wasn't me on the Jumbotron anymore.

It was her.

I nearly dropped my guitar.

The crowd reacted in waves. There were confused murmurs and excited shouts. My pulse pounded in my ears as I stared up at the screen.

She looked... breathless. Eyes wide, lips parted, hair slightly messy like she'd run through a storm to get here. Also, she appeared to be wearing some Mardi Gras beads and a feather boa.

And then she grabbed a handheld mic from the AV cart. "Logan," she said, her voice echoing into the stadium. "I'm sorry."

A sharp pang hit me in the chest. I yanked the mic back up to my mouth. "*Where* are you?" The crowd laughed, but I was dead serious.

Elizabeth glanced over her shoulder. "Uh... in the tech section?"

I squinted into the crowd but didn't see her. "I don't see you!" I called, throwing a hand in the air like a frustrated teacher. "Wave or something!"

She must have climbed onto a chair because I caught a flash of her, waving her arms.

"There!" I pointed. The camera zoomed in on her face.

The crowd roared.

Elizabeth, still standing precariously on the chair, adjusted the mic she'd somehow commandeered. "Can I talk now?"

I grinned despite the nervousness buzzing in my chest. "Please. And will you please get off that chair before you fall?"

She looked out at the crowd, took a deep breath, and carefully stepped down from the chair.

My hands twitched around my guitar. I was too far away to catch her if she slipped, but every muscle in me tensed like I could somehow cross the whole stadium in time if she wobbled.

She didn't. She stood tall, feet on solid ground, mic in hand.

The Superdome fell silent, the entire crowd holding their breath as she spoke.

"Logan," she started, her voice steady now. "I know I don't deserve another chance after everything. But I need you to know that I was wrong to walk away. I let my fear get the best of me, and I hurt you because I couldn't trust myself to let you in."

Every part of me ached hearing those words.

Elizabeth swallowed hard, then met my gaze through the camera lens. "But I've realized something. I don't want to be scared anymore. And I don't want to be without you. If you can forgive me, and if you'll have me, I'm here. For real this time."

The crowd erupted into cheers, but I barely heard them.

All I could hear was the echo of her voice in my ears, *If you'll have me.*

I snapped out of my daze and turned to the tech crew. "Get her up here!" I waved toward the press section like a lunatic.

They hesitated.

"Come on!" I shouted, more frantic now. "SOMEONE go get her!"

Security scrambled, parting the crowd like the Red Sea.

Elizabeth didn't wait. The second the mic cut out and the crowd erupted, she took off, jumping down from the raised tech platform. She ran through the crush of people on the floor, the crowd stepping aside to let her pass. At some point, she lost the feather boa, and to stop the Mardi Gras beads from jangling against her chest, she took them off and threw them to the people cheering her on.

By the time she reached the barricade in front of the stage, she was breathless and flushed. Security helped her onto the stage, and the roar of the crowd shook the Dome.

Elizabeth stood in front of me, still catching her breath, looking as gorgeous and stubborn as ever.

"Hi," I said into the mic, my heart pounding.

Her gaze softened. "Hi."

The crowd screamed.

I stepped closer, my voice quieter now. "You came."

She swallowed, her hands twisting together. "I... I was wrong, Logan, about everything. I was scared, and I let that ruin us. But I—" Her voice broke, and she took a deep breath. "I love you."

The noise of the crowd, the flashing lights, and the chaos of the night all blurred together.

All that mattered was her.

"Good," I said, pulling her into my arms. "Because I've been waiting for you."

And then, right there on stage in front of thousands of people, I kissed her.

The Superdome exploded into cheers, but all I cared about was Elizabeth—her hands tangling in my hair, her body pressing into mine, the way she sighed against my lips.

When we finally broke apart, I leaned into the mic, still holding her close.

"Actually," I murmured into the mic, letting my lips brush against her temple, "I take it back."

Elizabeth pulled back slightly, her brows furrowed. "Take what back?"

I turned to the audience, my grip tightening around her waist.

"This won't be the last time I sing this song," I said, my voice steady now. "I might be singing it every day for the rest of my life."

# EPILOGUE: ELIZABETH

**ONE YEAR LATER**

The animal charity's gala at City Park was in full swing, the evening alive with laughter, champagne bubbles, and the excited yips of puppies finding their forever homes. The twinkling string lights above us cast everything in a golden glow, making it feel like something straight out of a movie.

And in a way, it was.

Because once upon a time, this was the exact place I had orchestrated a ridiculous PR stunt—a fake first date that spiraled into one of the most absurd plans I'd ever hatched. I had put Sophie and Logan together in front of the cameras, all to convince the world that he was in a perfect relationship.

And now, I was standing here with him, and I was the one in the relationship. Not a perfect relationship, but a real one.

"Full circle," Logan murmured, his arm slung lazily around my shoulders as he surveyed the scene.

I tilted my head up to look at him, the warm glow of the gala lights catching in his dark eyes. "What do you mean?"

He smirked. "This is where it all started. The fake date. Sophie and I posing for the cameras, all kissy-kissy. While you stood off to the side, pretending you didn't care. But then, you just happened to 'accidentally' fall into my arms."

I laughed, shaking my head, playing along. "You're remembering that wrong. I tripped. Clearly. Because of Buttons. And because of you."

He raised an eyebrow. "Sure, yeah, you 'tripped.' Right into my arms. Convenient."

I rolled my eyes, as warmth flickered in my chest. "I can't believe you're blaming a poor, defenseless puppy to cover your smooth moves, Mr. Richards."

He flashed a grin. "Blaming? No way. I owe that dog a treat."

Then, before I could catch on to what he was doing, he nudged me toward a small puppy pen in the middle of the gala, where six playful, floppy-eared puppies were currently tumbling over each other.

"Come on," he said, grinning. "Let's meet our new puppy."

Inside the pen, a tiny, wriggling ball of fur barreled toward us, his tail wagging so hard his entire body moved with it. He looked just like his father, Buttons. The difference? This dog was ours.

Logan crouched to scoop him up. "Think he'll be as much trouble as his dad?"

"Worse," I said, grinning. "He's got us as parents."

The puppy licked his chin, then immediately tried to chew on my dress's hem. I reached out to scratch his ears, but Logan caught my hand, threading his fingers through mine. When I looked up, his expression had softened.

"This feels good, doesn't it?" he murmured. "Being here. Settling down for a while."

I nodded, my heart full. Logan had just finished his latest world tour—a massive success—and for the first time, we had time just to *be*. I'd joined him on the road whenever I could, soaking in late-night adventures and stolen moments between shows. But now, we were home.

The animal charity had done so well in the past year that they'd expanded to open a no-kill shelter on a sprawling farm in Mississippi. Their founder, Paula, had become one of my favorite clients, and I'd thrown myself into helping them grow.

"You know," Logan mused, standing up with the puppy still in his arms, "this gala might be a good excuse to come back here every year."

I smiled. "You don't need an excuse. This city's home."

Logan's gaze softened, his voice quieter now. "And so are you."

Before I could respond, he shifted the puppy to one arm and reached into his pocket.

And then he was dropping to one knee. The world seemed to stop as Logan looked up at me, the night air thick with anticipation.

"Elizabeth," he said, holding up a simple but stunning ring, "a year ago, I didn't think I'd ever get to stand here with you like this."

My breath caught in my throat.

"You showed me what it means to believe in someone," Logan continued, his voice steady despite the emotion behind it. "To fight for something real. And to build a life that's messy and chaotic and beautiful."

The puppy barked, squirming in his arms, and we both laughed.

"And now, I want you to be mine forever. Will you marry me?"

Tears blurred my vision as I nodded, unable to speak.

"Yes," I whispered, my voice shaky. "Of course."

He slipped the ring onto my finger and pulled me into a kiss, the sounds of the gala and the world around us melting away.

The puppy yipped in protest, wiggling between us, and we both laughed, breaking apart just enough to settle him. As we walked back toward the party, hand in hand, I couldn't help but reflect on how much had changed.

And it was true, Sophie and Lambert were still married. Turns out, they'd eloped at eighteen, and even though they filed for divorce, it had never gone through. Sophie thought Lambert had handled it. Lambert thought Sophie had handled it. Neither of them actually had. Now, they were blissfully happy. Lambert had even started a plumbing business catering exclusively to the rich and famous in Hollywood. It was called The Royal Flush.

Sarah and Jake had tied the knot in a ceremony as delightful as they were. The reception had a brass band and a gumbo station. The gene therapy medical trial that Jake was in showed promise in slowing the nerve degeneration in his legs. And last week, they announced that they were expecting their first child, a girl.

Mick had been at the wedding, grumbling the entire time, but it was impossible to ignore the way he had softened over the past year. He had become like a father to me.

As for Logan and me? We were building something solid. Something real. As we reached the edge of the party, he pulled me into a slow spin beneath the string lights, his lips brushing against my ear.

A year ago, I didn't know that love wasn't about control. That it wasn't about fixing things or managing outcomes.

It was about showing up.

It was about choosing someone, every single day, even when things got messy.

And with Logan, life promised to be nothing *but* messy. But it was the kind of mess I'd finally learned to welcome. The kind that meant living with your whole heart, even if it meant breaking it open sometimes. The kind that meant late-night arguments, early-morning laughter, and inside jokes no one else would ever understand. The kind that meant love, not the polished, filtered version, but the real, breathing, untidy kind.

We'd stumbled into this—backwards, sideways, wrapped in a leash and a lie.

And somehow, we'd found our way forward.

It started with a fake relationship.

But it ended with two people choosing each other for real.

## THE END

## Celebrity Love in New Orleans (complete series)

Scandalously Yours
Starfully Yours
Suddenly Yours
Secretly Yours
Suitably Yours (free novella)

## Thank You

In love with New Orleans? Sign up for my newsletter and get a free novella, Suitably Yours.

## About the Author

Katie Talbot writes romantic comedies about sassy, smart heroines. Her debut five-book series, *Celebrity Love in New Orleans,* is set in the city she calls home. Originally from Nebraska, she now lives in the Big Easy with her husband and three wonderful children.

# ACKNOWLEDGMENTS

First, I would like to thank my children—P, L, and MV. I'm proud and grateful to be your mother.

To P, our kids (and I) hit the jackpot with you. Thank you for being my biggest fan.

To my writing group, Amy Page, KC Newbury, and Elyse Haynes, who were instrumental in keeping me on track. Amy, you are the reason my books are crossing the finish line. I don't know how to thank you for your publishing expertise. KC, you're the plot whisperer and have been my motivator more than once. Elyse, you are my inspiration as a successful sweet rom-com writer, and your sunny sense of humor is second to none.

To every single person who read a draft, made suggestions, or cheered me on. Thank you.

To my editor, Whitney Jones of Empowered Writing, who did more than anyone else to whip this book into shape. Anything good you read in this book is probably due to her, though any errors are my own.

And to my readers: Thank you for giving this story a shot! I hope you laughed more than you rolled your eyes.

Stay smart, stay sassy,

Katie

www.ingramcontent.com/pod-product-compliance
Lightning Source LLC
Chambersburg PA
CBHW050837180626
46814CB00007B/2504